Dispatches

The Big Room
(with Guy Peellaert)

WALTER
WINCHELL

WALTER WINCHELL

A NOVEL

MICHAEL HERR

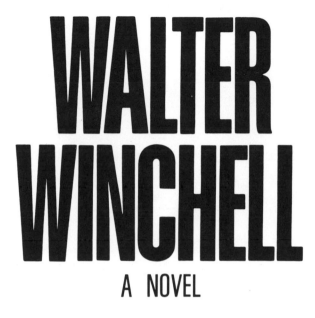

ALFRED A. KNOPF   *New York*   1990

THIS IS A BORZOI BOOK
PUBLISHED BY ALFRED A. KNOPF, INC.

Copyright © 1989, 1990 by MGM/UA Communications Company

A portion of this work was originally published in *Esquire*.

Grateful acknowledgment is made to CPP/Belwin, Inc., International
Music Publications, and Edward Brucker and Andrew G. Brucker as
trustees for the Florence and Edgar Leslie Charitable Foundation for
permission to reprint an excerpt from "America, I Love You" by Edgar
Leslie and Archie Gottler. Copyright 1915 by Mills Music, Inc.
Copyright renewed. Rights in the open market administered by
International Music Publications. All rights reserved. Used by
permission.

Library of Congress Cataloging in Publication Data

Herr, Michael.
    Walter Winchell : a novel / by Michael Herr.—1st
ed.
      p.   cm.
    "A Borzoi book."
    ISBN 0-394-58372-8
    1. Winchell, Walter, 1897–1972—Fiction.   I. Title.
PS3558.E73W35   1990
813'.54—dc20   89-43392
                                                                  CIP

Manufactured in the United States of America

FIRST EDITION

Preface

The book that you are about to read began its life as a screen-play, and no attempt has been made to conceal its origins from you. For reasons that were both practical and temperamental, it was written in prose instead of in standard screenplay form. In other words, its first intentions were cinematic, but its impulses and energies must have come from someplace else. To be honest, I always meant it to be read, and in that sense thought of it as something "more" than a screenplay. To compound this honesty, I have to add that its producers thought of it as something less than a screenplay. Having written it and grown used to it, I find this exercise in generic labeling not only awkward and distasteful, but very difficult.

Even though *Walter Winchell* is based on the life of a real man and often uses his actual words, it's a fiction, and it's in prose. So it must be a prose fiction. You could call it a screen-play that's typed like a novel, that reads like a novel but plays like a movie. Maybe it's a completely new form, or a wrinkle on an old form, or a mongrel. Maybe it's just a novel with a camera in it. Personally, my most ambitious claims for it are as an entertainment in the tradition of the Hollywood biopic, with the undertones of history spreading beneath the jokes in various bitter shades of dark.

What people refer to as "cinematic writing" in prose is called "literary" if it turns up in a script. Screenwriting is a discipline in which language is bound over in the service of images.

Descriptive writing in screenplays is more in the nature of a diagram than a narrative, notes to the director whose medium it really is. The writer can make all the suggestions he wants about the grading of emotion behind a given line, about physical business, costume, even lighting, but he can't make *mise en scène*. And whatever claims may be made for the power and beauty of short fragments arranged on the page to encapsulate long stretches of plot unfolding over passing time, montage is exclusive to the movies.

It's pretty obvious to me now that even from the beginning, when I thought I was thinking in pictures, I was really thinking in prose: a flat and telegrammatic prose, sometimes too abrupt to make a whole sentence, proceeding exclusively in the present tense, even in the flashbacks, something like Damon Runyon's prose in this respect, and for the same reason—it saves time. Instead of subordinating language to picture, I only sublimated it, and halfheartedly at that. I managed to form the language into scenes, most of them very short, and to float the scenes on dialogue; animated dialogue (I imagined), for the movies. But finally, dialogue is language too. In *Walter Winchell*, the dialogue *is* the action, or most of it. And while it might often say more than the character speaking it means to say, it's pretty external, or at least externalizing. "He says" and "She says" is a long way from "He thought" or "She felt." Winchell and Runyon and their circle were not particularly famous for their introspection. None of these people is Hamlet (except maybe the character called Ernest Hemingway), but they're tragic nonetheless.

On the night that this story begins, there were roughly 140 million Americans, 50 million of whom read Walter Winchell's newspaper column every day, six days a week, in over a thousand papers. An even greater number listened to his weekly radio broadcast. And if they could have been anywhere they wanted on this night, many of them would have chosen The Stork Club, as good a name as there will ever be for the glamour space *par excellence*, a place they only knew about through Walter Winchell, the wizard of the American vicarious: gossip columnist, failed vaudevillian, power broker, and journalistic demagogue, one of the most powerful and famous men of his time. That he is barely remembered today, and practically unheard of by anybody under forty, only gives his story a larger shape than the mere rise and slide and fall of his actual life. If passing time has obliterated him, it has also given him the status of a forgotten ancestor. If people go around today treating themselves like celebrities because not to be a celebrity is just too awful, we may have Walter Winchell to thank.

Because a story happened a long time ago, it's always a temptation to say that it happened in a more innocent time. The old days always look great, except possibly on film. With a few exceptions (*Barry Lyndon*, or *The Godfather*, or one of Martin Scorsese's fabulous screen poems of male hysteria), the past in the movies is rarely more than yellow filters, art directors' egos, and actors standing around in their wardrobe trying to breathe normally. What's supposed to be a foreign country looks far too local, exotic in all the wrong places. There's always a problem of running time in historical movies, and you need the clumsy apparatus of player identification, "Lenin, meet Trotsky," and characters telling each other things that we know they already know. The Word can take you back with much less effort.

You know that the gorgeous brunette dancing with Walter Winchell in The Stork Club is Hedy Lamarr because it says so on the page. If you don't remember exactly who Hedy

Lamarr was, you know at least that she was a gorgeous brunette, gorgeous enough to be a movie star. The same is true of the other historical figures in the book. Texas Guinan was a brash, careless woman who ran a nightclub; Owney Madden was a tough guy who ran New York; Mark Hellinger was a *bon vivant* of Broadway; Irving Hoffman a press agent with a heart of gold (and the closest thing that this particular Walter Winchell ever had to a conscience); Frank Costello was a suave gangster; Bernarr Macfadden an eccentric publisher; and so forth. It's simpler to consider these names as just the names of characters. They're all recognizable as types and, in true biopic style, that's how they're arranged and presented.

As for our hero, "that dreadful man," I don't mind imbuing his miserable history with a touch of glamour and even sympathy, as long as I don't have to defend him against charges of vulgarity. The public display of his life was raucous and incessant, while the private tariff ran on untabulated, unless maybe in the tentative approaches to intimacy that only occurred in the front seat of his car, during the brief entr'actes of his career, pursued through Harlem by the devils of yesterday's papers; or unremarked on, except from the sidelines and way out of earshot, by the sweaty little chorus of press agents, whose humiliation speaks for itself.

He was as nice to people as he had to be on the way up, and totally brutal coming down. It's amazing how many people there were who actually liked him even when they didn't have to, and how many there were who hated him but forgave him. He always knew that fate's natural and expected malice would do something awful to him, just as it had to all his friends. Stripped of his iconic power, the flags all fallen out of his map, he was left to look for whatever there was in himself that was most human; what we call human. They say (and I choose to believe) that at the end of his life, he became quite sweet-tempered and resigned to his losses. But then they also say that even after his death, there were plenty of people around who were still afraid of Walter Winchell.

WALTER WINCHELL

New York—1943

Late afternoon, East Fifty-third Street, in front of The Stork
Club. A man is washing the sidewalk with soap and water.
The doorman, in shirtsleeves, picks up some discarded newspapers from the curb. We see the canopy, the front doors with
the club logo—storks with top hats and canes—etched in the
glass. In the foyer, the logo is repeated in a mural along one
wall.

Inside The Stork Club. The cleaning staff is busy preparing
the club for the evening. The velvet rope beside the Reservations
Captain's station is being brushed, the brass posts that hold it
are being polished. Vacuum cleaners, polishing machines.

A CLEANING WOMAN is dusting the photographs on the wall
leading to the main room of the club. She comes to the
photograph of WALTER WINCHELL, hung in the most prominent
spot. We see him in the photo: hat on, coat off, sleeves rolled
up, sitting in front of an NBC microphone with his mouth
open. She dusts the photo, but leaves it slightly crooked.

A tall, well-dressed man, SHERMAN BILLINGSLEY, comes by,
carrying a sheaf of invoices. He sees the photograph, straight-
ens it.

"Five hundred people will walk past it tonight, and no one
will notice," he says. "He'll spot it the minute he comes in
the door. And I'll hear about it."

He looks at the photo, smiles sardonically, and folds his
hands, bowing.

"Salaami, salaami, ba-loney," he says.

An employee trots by. Billingsley stops him.

"It's balloon night," he says. He takes an envelope from his pocket, counts out ten crisp hundred-dollar bills, and hands them to the employee.

The RESERVATIONS CAPTAIN is on the phone, hovering over his book.

"One moment, please, sir," he says. He nods to Billingsley. "A Mr. Feinstein, boss," he says.

"Mr. Feinstein is who?" Billingsley says.

"No one. Just Plain Feinstein."

"We have nothing for tonight," Billingsley says. Then, half to himself, "Too many Jews in here as it is."

Dusk, in front of The Stork Club. A New York *Daily Mirror* delivery van goes by. On the side is a large advertisement featuring WALTER WINCHELL's name and face.

In a room off the kitchen, the employee is rolling the hundred-dollar bills tightly, placing them inside balloons, and blowing the balloons up with a helium cylinder.

Billingsley, in the lobby, stops the HAT-CHECK GIRL as she walks to her counter. Her hair is worn in the peekaboo style popularized by Veronica Lake.

"Change your hair, Betty."

"What, now, Mr. B.?" she says.

"Right now."

The camera moves through the main room into a smaller room, the Cub Room. In a corner is a large banquette, TABLE 50. The table is bare. A crisp white tablecloth is snapped open, floating over the table as the OPENING CREDITS begin. We hear a lushly orchestrated "Autumn in New York." In succeeding shots, the table is elaborately prepared: places set for six or seven people; ashtrays; a telephone is polished and plugged in. In the lobby, the velvet rope is placed across the entrance and secured; the orchestra moves to the stand. A few early customers enter the club. At Table 50, a pad and some pencils are laid by the telephone. Some messages are placed. As the credits end, one last touch: a glistening orchid is placed on the table, so fresh that it practically shivers.

(NOTE: *In the following long passage, The Stork Club itself is featured as prominently as Winchell, Runyon, and so on, since it is the absolute center of the time and place over which Winchell holds such power. In this sequence, it is a not-too-obviously stylized Stork Club, the glamour heightened. When we see it in subsequent scenes, it will have little of this atmosphere; when we see it depicted in earlier times, it will seem almost neutral. But on this night, at its peak, it is infused with glamour.*

Similarly, the characters featured in this sequence are men at the height of their attainments. What we see in WINCHELL, RUNYON, BILLINGSLEY, *and* HEMINGWAY *is the strenuously controlled artificial public comportment of four very complicated, powerful, selfish, and lonely men: three writers and an ex-gangster.*

RUNYON: *The complete cynic. He seems really to care for no one, although something warm flickers along the bond connecting him to Winchell.*

BILLINGSLEY: *He's not exactly rough around the edges. The edges are smooth enough, but something very rough remains lodged deeply at his center.*

HEMINGWAY: *Already far gone in believing his public image; self-conscious, vain, extremely sensitive, half crazy. By far the most refined of the four men, and the most sophisticated. He has broken through the wall of cynicism that contains the others.*

They've seen the very worst in people, and are always ready to believe the worst.

The personnel at Table 50 changes frequently. There is a steady stream of anonymous visitors, supplicants, etc. Some stay long enough to accomplish their business with Winchell and leave; some join the table for a few moments. They are unidentified and undifferentiated. They speak the odd line: "Somebody says." Among the press agents, only IRVING HOFF-MAN *is featured.*

The dialogue, particularly Winchell's semi-uninterrupted monologue, is swift. Some of it should overlap, setting the precedent for overlapping items that will be heard later during the scenes of Walter broadcasting, and giving the sense that nobody interrupts Winchell except Winchell. Between bits and scenes at Table 50, we see the life of The Stork Club on this particular evening.)

Midnight, The Stork Club. The Cub Room is packed, the dance floor is crowded, the orchestra playing "People Will Say We're in Love." Many of the couples on the floor are quite young, although some are middle-aged. Some are bored, some drunk, some dancing mechanically, by rote; middle-aged men with young women, a few older women with young men. One young couple is dancing passionately, kissing almost violently. Everyone is beautifully, expensively dressed. Even the military uniforms seem tailored. People look openly at the camera, happy and unself-conscious.

The camera moves rapidly from the front doors of the club through the crowds, Walter Winchell's p.o.v., people turning as though they've felt a blast of tremendous energy at their backs; smiling, greeting, recognizing him with pleasure and

even awe. His voice explodes on the sound track in full an-
ecdotal cry, two hundred words per minute, and is heard
uninterrupted for a few moments. Sometimes it's heard loose,
against random images; sometimes it's in real connection with
what he is saying at Table 50. The telephone on the table
buzzes frequently, and he switches his talk to it, rapidly making
notes with his left hand on the pads provided for him.

The camera moves to the sidewalk outside to show taxis and
limousines arriving; people moving past the knot of gawkers
on the street; the velvet rope is let down and refastened. A
DRUNK is rushed smoothly but firmly out of the club. As he
goes, protesting his solvency, he throws fifty-dollar bills behind
him.

Billingsley moves around the rooms, in and out of the
kitchen, past the bar, watching everything and everyone like
a hawk. A strange, not particularly warm smile is fixed on his
face. It barely alters as people greet him, as he welcomes
customers, as he speaks to a HANDSOME COUPLE entering the
Cub Room.
"Hiya, Sherman," the man says.
"Hi, kids. Been to the theatre?"
"And how! Have you seen *Oklahoma*?"
"Seen it?" Billingsley says. "I was born there."
And above this activity, cutting through it, is Winchell's
voice:
"God, I love this country," Walter says. "You say that
around Broadway, they look at you like they're waiting for the
punch line, but I don't care, that's how I feel. The day we got
into the war in 1917 I gave up everything and joined the Navy."
"What everything?" Runyon says.
"That's the point," Walter says. "I loved America then,

when I had nothing. Now that I have everything, I love her even more."

"Naturally," Runyon says.

"Walter loves America from Forty-second Street all the way up to the Park," someone says.

"Aw baloney," Walter says. "It never ceases to amaze me how people get things wrong . . . The misconceptions are staggering . . . Everybody thinks I'm just a Broadway guy but I bet there isn't a burg in this whole country I haven't been in at least once . . . Join vaudeville and see the world . . . When I had the Winchell and Greene act, we used to buy European labels to stick on our luggage . . . The hotels treated you like bums if you didn't have them."

"Weren't you and Greene married?" somebody says.

"None of your business," Walter says. "That's private. And anyway, don't interrupt."

Walter is seated in the middle at Table 50. Next to him is Damon Runyon. There are a few others sitting with them, transients.

". . . You can't believe what it's like out there, jerkwater towns, you ask some local, Where's the theatre? . . . Dunno. Okay, where's the train station? . . . Dunno . . . Well, where do you *live*? . . . Dunno. Strictly from Mortimer Snerd . . . God, they're dumb out there."

The phone buzzes. "Yeah. I already know that. Then what are you wasting my time for?" He slams the phone down. "Jerk."

A man approaches the table and hands Walter an envelope, which he opens immediately.

"Georgie-Porgie, whaddya got?" he says. "Did you hear the broadcast Sunday?"

"I'm sorry, Walter, I missed it. My mother died Sunday morning."

"That's no excuse," Walter says. He reads the item. "Heh heh heh. 'She got her mink coat the hard way—her husband gave it to her.' That's good, Georgie."

"Thanks, Walter."

"Keep it up." The man goes.

"Look at this," Walter says, showing Runyon the stationery. Across the top is printed *Exclusive to Walter Winchell.* "George doesn't want me to think he does business with my competition, as if I had any. I call those other guys my wastebasket. If it isn't good enough for Winchell, it's plenty good enough for them . . . Where was I?"

"You were talking about yourself," Runyon says.

"Oh, yeah . . . The road . . . I got out just in time. I woulda been a headliner, but I could see vaudeville was on its last legs . . . Who needs it? Anyway, I wanted to be a newspaperman."

"And how did it work out, Walter?" Runyon says.

"Verra fonya, Damon. I write the news six days a week. Fifty million people read it in a thousand newspapers. And Runyon says I'm not a newspaperman."

"You're *not* a newspaperman," Runyon says.

"No? What am I then?" Walter says, enjoying it.

"You're something more and less than a newspaperman."

"Damon's been sticking me with that same needle for twenty years, ever since I came into this racket. He was just a sportswriter then. Everybody was saying, 'You got to read Runyon, you got to read Runyon.' I said, What for? I *hate* sports. But I read him. I learned something from it, too."

"Only thing Walter ever learned from me was how to fill out expense accounts," Runyon says.

"This was before Runyon made his first million," Walter says, eager to carry on his monologue.

"I wasn't trying . . ."

"Wasn't trying . . . You just hadn't heard of Hollywood then."

"Well," Runyon says. "You make it there and you spend it here."

Walter (impatient at being interrupted, even by Runyon) takes firm command of the conversation.

"Remember that shmatte, the *Vaudeville News*? When I started there, they were giving it away. *Giving* it away! Can you believe those shmucks?"

His telephone buzzes. He picks it up, says, "Yea," and continues talking to the table with his hand over the mouthpiece. "I said, charge a nickel for it, make me advertising manager, I'll review plays, do a column, sell ads, and keep twenty percent. Three months, I was making more than the editor. . . ." He uncovers the telephone mouthpiece, says, "Okay," and hangs up. "Twenty years, and look at me now! When I first met Runyon, I was still more of a song-and-dance man than a reporter."

"Still are," Runyon says.

"And did Damon give me the high hat! The old frosteroo. I was too brash for him."

"Brash!" Runyon says. "That's a pretty word for it. You were impossible. And also, remember—you were a nobody then."

"And nobody loves a nobody," Walter says, beaming.

"But nobody," Runyon says.

"So I'm not a newspaperman, so listen to this," Walter says, whipping a piece of paper from his pocket. "From the Columbia University *Journalism Review*, yet: '*He* [Walter jams his thumb into his chest],' meaning me, folks, 'has done more to rouse the consciousness of America against intolerance and totalitarianism than any other *journalist* of his time.' "

"And made more money doing it, too," Runyon says.

But Walter's attention is suddenly fixed on a middle-aged

woman across the room. "My God," he says. "Look at her! What happened to her?"

"How old is she?" someone asks.

"I don't know," Walter says. "But she'll never live to be as old as she looks."

Billingsley passes the table.

"Hey, Sherman," Walter says, "I hear that putz Ed Sullivan was sneaking in here while I was in Florida."

"He was in here every night," Billingsley says. "I gave him your table, too."

"That's cute, Sherm," Walter says, but Billingsley has fixed on a WAITER who is passing through the room on his way to the kitchen. Billingsley follows him, a look of sinister purpose on his face.

Just inside the kitchen, Billingsley stops him.

"Hey, Cabriola."

"Yes, boss."

"A little birdie tells me you joined the union. Is this true, Guinea-ola?" He starts shoving the waiter as he talks. "I don't pay you enough? You don't make enough in tips? You don't *steal* enough? You go and join the *fucking union* on me?"

"I got a right," the Waiter says weakly.

"You gotta right?" Billingsley says. "*You* gotta right, *I* gotta right. You're through. Now. Get out of my club." Then, quite calmly, almost as an afterthought, he punches the waiter hard in the face. As the man falls back against the wall, Billingsley starts to laugh, a strange, cold laugh. He's still laughing as he joins Table 50.

"What's the gag?" Walter says. "Can I use it?"

"No gag," Billingsley says. "Something just struck me funny." Spotting a familiar face beyond the table, he says hello.

·   ·   ·

A large bearded man, ERNEST HEMINGWAY, strides to Table 50, pursued by the maître d', who is muttering apologies. "Verra sorry, Meester Heminvay," etc. Hemingway is dressed in a rough tweed suit, a carelessly knotted tie, and a checked shirt.

"That's okay," Hemingway says to the maître d'. "Just for Christ's sake please stop apologizing, will you?" He greets Walter and Damon. "Hello, Commander. Colonel Runyon."

"Ernie Hemorrhoid, the poor man's Pyle," Winchell says. "Jesus, will you look at that tan . . . You have some trouble at the door?"

"I seem to be in some violation of the dress code," Hemingway says.

"Well, wardrobe is important around here," Damon says. "Sherman fired one of his captains for letting a man in here wearing white socks. And who's to say he was wrong?"

"Any man who wears white socks after five o'clock deserves whatever he gets," Hemingway says. He pulls up a trouser leg. He's wearing moccasins, and no socks at all.

A nervous man approaches Table 50. Winchell holds up his hand. "Unh-uh," he says sharply.

"Aw, Walter," the man says.

"Beat it, or I'll have Sherman throw you out on your ass. . . . Go on. Waltz, waltz."

The man leaves. The camera makes another move around the room, one orchestra tune fades into another, a half hour has passed.

"Cary Grant is Jewish," Walter is saying. "Sure he's Jewish."

"He certainly keeps it to himself," Billingsley says.

"No, no, on the contrary. He's always saying it, but no one wants to listen. Louella, Hedda, they can't even hear him, but it's true. Pure Yidloch."

"Well, he doesn't look Jewish," Billingsley says.

"Whadda you know from Jewish, Sherm? I took Sherman to Lindy's one night. He thought the waiters were speaking Japanese. He wanted me to report them to Johnny Hoover. He ordered a pastrami on raisin bread with ketchup."

"There weren't too many Hebrews out where Sherman and I come from," Runyon says.

"What, no Jewish cowboys?" Walter says.

"Are you kidding?" Billingsley says. "Cowboys only earn thirty dollars a month."

A waiter places a shrimp cocktail in front of Billingsley. He picks up a fork and then stops, staring unhappily at it. He looks puzzled.

"Tell the chef I want a word with him," he says to the waiter. "What's wrong with this?" he demands of Winchell, Runyon, and Hemingway. They all shrug. The CHEF comes up.

"What's wrong with this?" he asks the Chef.

"Looks fine to me, Mr. B.," the chef says.

"Looks fine to me, too," Walter says. "I'll eat it if you don't want it."

"No," Billingsley says, troubled. "Something . . . something's not quite right. . . ."

"I'm sorry," the Chef says. "I think it's fine."

"This sounds like a Dutch comedy act," Walter says.

Billingsley quickly counts the shrimp. ". . . five, *six*. That's it! It's not big enough. From now on, I want seven shrimp in the shrimp cocktail."

"Right, boss," the Chef says.

"Make sure everybody knows."

"Sure, boss." The Chef leaves.

"It never ends," Sherman Billingsley says, smiling his private, distracted smile.

.   .   .

Time lapse, Winchell's voice:

"People always ask me, How did one man ever get so powerful? I tell them, plenty of hard work and plenty of common sense. You didn't have to be a genius to figure out that we were gonna have a war with the Nazis . . . *Oiving!*

. . . Franklin Roosevelt, God bless him, thinks my grasp of the international situation is phenomenal, but I just tell him what I'm . . . *Oiving! Over here!* . . . What I'm telling you . . ."

As he talks, he's signaling to a man in the doorway of the Cub Room, Irving Hoffman; a middle-aged, myopic man, with an ATTRACTIVE YOUNG WOMAN.

"Oh, Oi-ving," Walter calls. "He can hear me but he can't see me. Blind as a frigging bat . . . Douglas MacArthur said the same thing the President said. He never misses a column or a broadcast. He wanted me to come to Washington to go over the . . . Irving, come, sit. You know these people?"

Irving sort of squints at the table. "Probably," he says. "Hello, Walter. This is Susan Raymond, spelled the usual way. Tell me, Walter, how's Junie?" The way Hoffman asks this indicates a degree of close personal knowledge of Winchell, a degree of intimacy that no one else here quite has. There is also just a touch of gentle reproach.

"June's fine," Walter says. "She's wonderful."

"So where've you been hiding her?" Irving says.

"Behind his money," Runyon says.

"She's in Scarsdale," Walter says.

"You should spend more time there," Irving says.

"Are you kidding?" Walter says. "The nights are six months long in Scarsdale!"

Irving leans over and, indicating his date, asks Walter quietly, "Is she pretty, Walter?"

"I don't know who picks them for you, but you should let them buy your neckties, too," Walter says.

The orchestra starts to play a rhumba.

"Gotta dance, gotta dance . . . May I, Oiving . . . Do you rhumba, Miss Raymond?"

"Yes I do, Mr. Winchell," Susan says.

"Well, shoot the chassis to me, lassie . . ."

On the dance floor, Walter is mildly exhibitionistic, totally unrelaxed. Dancing all his life hasn't really made him a dancer; lots of energy, not much real grace. He's in a world of his own, excluding his partner, who is only a kind of reflector of his ego. The best you can say about his dancing is that he knows how to appear with a good-looking woman on a public floor.

The rhumba ends. Returning to the table, Walter spots a MAN. "Hey, Howard," he calls.

"Don't speak to me, you rattlesnake," Howard says.

"What's the matter with *you?*" Walter says. "I spelled your name right, didn't I?"

Howard keeps going.

"Remember, Howard," Walter calls, taunting. "Every knock a boost."

A YOUNG COUPLE greet him as he approaches his table.

"Walter, we're having a baby," the Man says.

"Great. Who do you suspect?"

"Oh, Walter," they laugh, slightly fawning. As soon as he returns to the table, Walter jots this down. We see him write the word "infanticipating."

Runyon is talking to Hemingway: "For real class, you can't beat Babe Ruth. He was at a formal dinner party, fifty people, a footman behind every chair, and the servingman offers him a silver tray with asparagus. 'No thanks,' the Babe says. 'It makes my urine smell funny.' "

Time lapse. Walter talking: "I hear Bill Fields is a very sick man."

"Well, the way *he* drinks . . ." Damon says.

"He and Johnny Barrymore," Walter says. "I never saw anything like it in my life, the booze."

"I had to throw Barrymore out of here one night," Billingsley says.

"Haw, you loved it," Walter says. "One night Johnny and I went home with three showgirls . . . Cover your pretty little ears, Susan . . . One for me, one for him, and one to cover the outfield. They hadda work hard with John, he was always so shikker. He used to say, 'Ah, Walter—so many women, and so little time . . .' "

"He never called them 'women' in his life," Damon says. "He called 'em 'pancakes.' Or 'squab.' "

"Well, rest in peace," Walter says. "He was always a lot of fun. (At this point, Irving leans over and begins to speak softly to Susan.) Unlike his goddamned sister. Ethel Barrymore once said (he uses a haughty falsetto), 'I don't see why Walter Winchell is allowed to live.' " Walter glares at Irving, who is still whispering. "Pain in the ass, that broad. Irving, you're not listening."

The phone buzzes. "Whaddya mean, I got it wrong? *You* got it wrong. I know all about it. Don't call me again, you chiseler . . . So who gives two shits? Drop dead!" He slams down the phone.

"I'm telling you, this frigging game. They only ask you two questions: Why did you print that? and Why didn't you print that? Nobody trusts you, your family hates you, you ruin your health, and when it's all over, if you have a single friend left, it's a miracle. Go be a reporter!"

"A good reporter is the noblest work of God," Hemingway says.

"Why, thank you, Ernest," Walter says.

"Kipling said that," Hemingway says.

"Walter doesn't know who Kipling is," Damon says.

"He: Do you like Kipling? She: I don't know. I never kippled," Walter says.

"There you are, gentlemen," Runyon says.

"Boots, boots, boots, boots . . . I know the guy you mean," Walter says.

"Ever read my stuff?" Hemingway asks.

"Every book. Every word. I love it. Short sentences. Like my stuff," Walter says.

"I studied under Colonel Runyon," Hemingway says.

"No one can teach me any tricks about keepin' 'er short," Damon says.

"How come you never use the past tense in your stories?" Hemingway asks.

"I don't know," Damon says. "Saves time, I reckon."

"Me, I use three dots," Walter says. "Dot dot dot. Fast dots . . . Lean."

"I still say Walter never read a book in his life," Runyon says.

"He's absolutely right," Hemingway says. "Books are for saps."

Time lapse. Conga line on dance floor, Walter's voice at Table 50:

". . . Sinatra's getting thirty-five hundred a week at the Paramount. Not bad for a skinny little Italian kid from Hoboken. And you oughtta see him *eat*. He was in this spaghetti joint on Forty-third, packing it away like a three-hundred-pounder . . ."

Time lapse.

". . . so this guy orders his date a chicken sandwich and a whiskey and soda. But I want a steak and champagne, she says. Is that what your mother feeds you? No, she says, but my mother doesn't keep trying to put her hand between my legs."

Time lapse. Walter on the phone.

"Good. That's good. Call my secretary tomorrow. Tell her I told you to tell her to tell me."

Runyon gives him a look. Walter hangs up.

"There's never enough time, never enough time," he says. "I'm only getting five hours' sleep a night."

"Edison only got four," Irving says.

"Yeah. But Edison didn't have a column to get out."

Time lapse.

". . . Toby Carter, what a meshugge," Walter is saying. "He moved into a whorehouse in San Francisco for a week. He spent eight thousand dollars, and he never got laid."

"Did he get kissed?" Irving says. He and Susan are leaving.

"Where are you gonna be later on, Oiving?"

"Asleep. Please give June my love. You be a good boy, Walter."

Hemingway's attention is absorbed by a scene at a table across the room: A handsome young man is crying uncontrollably at the table. Walter notices Hemingway's fascination.

"He got his draft notice this morning," Walter says. "*After* his father gave the head of his draft board a new Studebaker, too. Frederick Ewell III—that family's been in so many messes they have a mop on their coat of arms."

"This war must be a great inconvenience for some," Hemingway says. "Walter, is it true that you have The Stork Club wired?"

"Ernesto, I got the whole town wired. I know all about it. I know who's doin' what to who, how long they've been doing it, how much they're doing it for, the where, the when, the how, the who hit Nelly in the belly with a flounder . . . I know."

"I bet I know more secrets than you do," Damon says. "I keep mine."

"I got a few," Walter says.

A very drunk woman comes up to the table. She has a black eye.

"Look, Walter," she whines. "Look what that crumbum did to me. I said, What about that item Walter ran about you and Ruthie Walters, and he threw an ashtray at me . . . you put *that* in your column, Walter."

"I will," Walter says.

"And say *I* told you. We'll fix that son of a bitch."

She weaves away.

"All this glamour is starting to pall," Runyon says.

Time lapse. Walter on the phone.

"Shmuckelheimer," Walter is saying. "You trying to louse me up? You don't say? You *don't* say? You better be." He hangs up. "I don't get paid for writing a column. I get a salary for being polite to pests."

The Captain comes over and mutters something in Billingsley's ear.

"Absolutely not," Billingsley says.

"He promises to be good," the Captain says.

"It's that pain in the ass Humphrey Bogart," Billingsley says to the table. He turns to the Captain. "Tell him when I'm dead, he can come in here anytime. Never mind. I'll tell him myself." He leaves the table.

"Sherman's just a tired businessman," Runyon says.

"He always looked like a pimp to me," Hemingway says.

"Well," Runyon says, "if you pulled his sheet and read back far enough, you'd probably find something to explain that feeling."

"Never," Walter says. "Sherman never pimped. He bootlegged. He may have killed a man or two. He's introduced people to other people, but that's always been in line with his duties as proprietor of The Stork Club, strictly for the good will."

"Besides," Hemingway says, "no gentleman would ever . . . A real gentleman could never . . . that's the sort of thing you wouldn't find a gentleman involved in." We notice that he's quite tight.

"Sherman's a gentleman?" Walter says.

"You couldn't *buy* manners like his," Damon says.

"Jesus," Walter says, staring at the dance floor. "Will you look at that woman dance."

We see an incredibly sexy woman dancing, time passing, Walter talking:

"I was back in uniform the day after Pearl Harbor, those morons in Congress hated me for it. They hated it that I was right, I'd been right all along and they couldn't stand it. I wanted active duty, too, but F.D.R. wouldn't have it. 'Walter,' he said, 'you're far too valuable to America to go to sea.' "

"And far too valuable to F.D.R.," Runyon says.

"And what's wrong with that?" Walter says, quite emotional.

"I'm proud. I'm proud to serve Franklin Roosevelt any way I can. He's the greatest president since Lincoln. God bless him. I'd give my life for Franklin Roosevelt." (We get the feeling that he means this.)

"Yeah, and he'd do the same for you," Runyon says.

"*Someone's* got to look out for the little people," Walter says.

"The *little* people?" Runyon says.

"Ugh," Billingsley says. "I can't stand them."

"We need them," Runyon says. "I admit we've got to have them. But between you and me, I don't want them anywhere near me. And that goes double for underdogs."

"So how come you voted for Roosevelt three times?" Walter says.

"I like the way he dresses," Runyon says. "Personally, I'd rather meet a heavyweight champion than a president any time."

"Any good boys around?" Hemingway asks.

"Not as many since they tried to clean up the game. Far as I'm concerned, there's nothing better than a good fixed fight. It requires a lot more finesse than the real thing. It's just as thrilling for the crowd, and it saves a lot of wear and tear on the boys. I like to know beforehand when the fix is in, so I can go and study the technique. Were you at the fights tonight?"

"No," Hemingway says. "We went to the ballet."

"The ballet?" Walter says.

"That's right?"

"So how was the footwork?" Walter says.

"Peggy Taylor, remember her, Sherman?"

"A doll," Sherman says.

"She almost married the Atwater Kent money last year . . .

that was good money, too . . . She's working as the cigarette girl at the French Casino now."

"C'est la guerre," Damon says.

"Maybe she didn't love him," Hemingway says.

"She must have not loved him very much, then," Damon says. "She ignored the cardinal rule of life: Get the money."

"I find that it can't buy happiness," Hemingway says, with deep conviction and absolute sincerity.

"It *is* happiness," Runyon says. "A good position at the feed trough. . . . Everything else is the phidinkus."

Walter is ravenously attacking a steak, when an UNCTUOUS MAN comes to the table.

"Walter, what can I say? That was very sweet of you," he says.

"Wha'?" Walter says, looking up, confused.

"It was my mother's birthday, and guess who sent her flowers?" the Man says. "Walter, they were just beautiful."

"Aw, don't mention it." The Man leaves.

"*I* did that?" Walter says.

"It certainly doesn't sound like you," Sherman says.

"It certainly doesn't," Walter says.

"Half the waiters in here used to own their own clubs during Prohibition," Walter is saying. "Hey, Dominic—didn't you use to own a nightclub?"

"Not me, Mr. Winchell," the waiter says. "I own eleven apartment houses."

A man comes to the table.

"Approach with caution," Walter says.

"No, it's okay," the man says. "It's a sure thing. Rita Hayworth is definitely pregnant."

"Yeah? First she is, then she isn't, now she is."

"Maybe she's just a little pregnant," Damon says.

"Well, Walter," the man says, "you can't stop her from having a baby."

"I can stop her from having it in my column."

The man leaves.

"*That's* Rita Hayworth's press agent?" Damon asks.

"Don't be ridic," Walter says. "Rita wouldn't wipe her shoes on that shmegegge. He fed me a wrongo a few weeks ago, and he's working off the penalty. Five or six free items, and I'll start plugging his clients again."

"Is that how it works?" Hemingway says.

"Yeah. It's tough, but it keeps them honest."

"Honest as a press agent," Runyon says. His voice seems to be growing hoarse.

"Your voice going on you, Damon?" Walter says.

"Yeah. I'm getting laryngitis from listening to you."

A drum roll, crash of cymbals, the orchestra starts playing an up-tempo "We're in the Money"; an incredible, almost infantile excitement spreads through the crowd as the orchestra leader yells, "Balloon Time!"

Hundreds of balloons are released. They float across the crowd as people clutch wildly after them, seizing them, bursting them with their hands, with cigarettes, stabbing them with forks. A woman, hysterical, is trying to hold a ridiculous number of balloons under her arms, under her chin, between her legs, while her dress slips from her shoulders. The orchestra segues into "The William Tell Overture" as two men pull at the same balloon. Occasionally there is a scream of delight: "I got one!"; people waving hundred-dollar bills over their heads. Others groan and curse with disappointment. Some people remain seated, aloof, disdainful. Hemingway looks on with incredible sadness. Walter is on the phone. Runyon watches with a mixture of distaste and satisfaction. "Get the money," he mutters, half to himself.

It is all over in a minute.

The street in front of The Stork Club. Many people are drifting out. We hear music coming through the doors. We see Hemingway walking up the street, alone, lost in thought.

Inside, on the dance floor, Walter is dancing a fox trot with a beautiful brunette, HEDY LAMARR.

"Does he want to marry you?" he says.

"He tells me that he does, if his wife will give him a divorce."

"And do you want to marry him?"

She smiles, dances a little closer to Walter. Then her expression changes; surprise, amusement, embarrassment, even pleasure. "Walter!" she says.

"What? . . . Oh," he says. He moves away from her and takes a Colt .38 out of his pocket. Dominic, the waiter, is passing the edge of the dance floor.

"Hey Dominic, give this to Runyon to hold for me, will you?"

"Sure thing, Mr. Winchell," Dominic says without batting an eye.

"Sorry, Hedy," Walter says. "You were saying . . ."

"I think I want to marry him. But I think I love John, too."

"This sounds familiar."

"Can you be in love with two people at the same time?" Hedy says.

"At least," Walter says. Something flickers over his face, as though his thoughts are on a dangerous threshold. "Love's a funny thing," he says. "A man bites a girl's neck because he thinks she has pretty legs."

The song ends, they return to the table. Only Runyon is left. Sitting down again, Walter spots a man across the room.

"Louie! Louie! C'mere!"

We see LOUIE. He looks angry. "You want to talk to me, you come over here."

Louie turns away from him.

"I think Louie's mad at you," Runyon says. "What did you do?"

Walter, somewhat resigned, vaguely ashamed, smirks.

"I've been a b-a-a-a-d boy," he says.

We see The Stork Club, empty now except for the cleaning crew. Most of the lights are off, the tables piled up, etc. CUT TO:

Harlem streets, 2 a.m. "The Flight of the Bumblebee" is heard as Winchell's black Ford speeds through the streets. Police calls crackle on the car radio.

Walter is driving. Hedy Lamarr is beside him, sleepy, resting her head on his shoulder. Runyon sits next to her. Zoot-suited Negroes stand on the corners, watching the car pass.

"I drive up here almost every night when I'm in town," Walter says. "Call me sentimental, but I always get a kick out of it."

They stop for a red light. A NEGRO MAN turns from his friends and looks at the car with sinister amusement.

"What you doin' up here, white man?" he says.

"I was born here, Rochester," Walter says.

"Yeah? Me too, Chuck," the Negro says.

"Maybe we're related," Walter says, as the light changes and he moves on.

"Hard to believe this was ever a Jewish neighborhood," Damon says.

"Shvartzehs follow Jews," Walter says. "It's the American way . . . Right here, see this building? I was up here a few years ago with Darryl Zanuck and Madeleine Carroll. A barber and his tootsie were having a big argument on the stoop there. The neighbors called the cops. When they got here, the barber was holding the girl in his arms, singing to her. They went to pick her up, and her head rolled down the stairs."

"My God," Hedy says.

"I'll bet they were surprised," Runyon says.

"Yeah, I'll bet they were at that," Walter says. "We were living over there when my old man took a powder on us. My grandmother had a candy store there, where the dry cleaners is. That was my Stork Club. All the yentas used to come in there to swap items.

"One thing I'll say for vaudeville," Walter says, "it got me out of this. Twelve years old . . . That's when I learned to write a column, sending postcards to my mother."

"Only twelve," Hedy says wistfully. "Weren't you homesick, Walter?"

Walter gives her an incredulous look, as though he thinks the question is insane.

He steps on the gas and the car speeds on, stirring up old newspapers that seem to cluster and fly after the car. . . .

We see the store, circa 1908; old women dressed in black speaking rapidly in Yiddish. Walter's GRANDMOTHER looks over the counter, sees WALTER, a little boy, hunched up behind it, eavesdropping. Grabbing him by the ear, she yanks him up and takes him out the door, while the women laugh.

. . .

Same street, same hour, 1910.

A man, Walter's FATHER, furtive and nervous, carrying a suitcase.

Walter's voice: "There's nothing wrong with poverty, except it's so damn boring. We were all poor, everyone we knew was poor. And boy, were we ashamed of it. Hustle, hustle, hustle. All that stuff about the noble poor is just the acamaracus."

"Amen," Runyon's voice says.

Over this, we see Walter, ten years old, standing by the IRT exit in the rain with an umbrella, trying to sell its protection to people for a nickel.

Walter, selling newspapers, running, tummeling, calling headlines.

Walter, working in a butcher shop. The butcher tosses him a filthy rag, and Walter wipes the blood from the meat hooks.

Runyon's voice: "I met a fella who says he went to school with you."

Walter's voice: "That's a good one. I never went to school."

We see young Walter sneaking into a vaudeville theatre. He watches the acts (Weber & Fields, Bill Robinson, Pat Rooney, Sr.), totally engrossed, with hungry, burning eyes.

A tenement hall bathroom. Walter, with the door locked, is practicing tap-dance steps, while a neighbor bangs on the door.

On the street, surrounded by extremely tough kids, he is humming and singing "The Daughter of Rosie O'Grady," accompanying his own hysterical tap dancing. He's terrible, but the kids are impressed.

Overhead, high above the rooftops, we see a tremendous

box kite, with a dummy on a trapeze hanging from it, and a long, gaudy banner advertising a show floating behind.

A theatre. In front of the orchestra pit, a card reading *The Little Men with the Big Voices*; Walter and two other boys are singing "Pony Boy." Walter's in show business.

Another card; *Gus Edwards' School Days.*
Walter's voice: "First headliner I ever knew. First guy who really had the dough, Gus Edwards. He had it coming and going. From his songs, from the act, he had a million bucks. And he paid us bubkes. He was smart."
We see the act, obviously big time. Ten children, all around twelve years old, dressed as school kids, and GUS EDWARDS as the teacher.
Pandemonium on stage, the kids running around yelling. Faster and louder than the rest, Walter, with a rolled-up newspaper, as THE BULLY, is hitting the other children on the head. Edwards appears onstage.
"Children, children . . . What's going on here? Can't I leave the room for two seconds?"
"It's Walter, teacher!" they cry. "It's his fault!"
"Why, ya liddle snitches," Walter snarls.
"Is this true, Walter?" Edwards says.
"Yes, teacher," Walter says, in a complete travesty of contrition.
"Well well. And what have you got to say for yourself?"
Grotesquely, in close-up, the face of a depraved cherub, "I'm a b-a-a-a-d boy."
"I really don't know what to do with you, Walter. Say, weren't you a Thanksgiving baby?"
"Yes, teacher."
"You were born on Thanksgiving Day?"

"Yes, teacher."

"Then your parents have a lot to be thankful for, haven't they?"

"Yeah. They're thankful I ain't twins."

This gets a big laugh from the audience.

"Hey, teacher," Walter says. "Is it true that you're a public servant?"

"Why, yes. I am a public servant."

"Then how about bringin' me a glass of water," Walter says, as the audience howls. We see that he is in ecstasy; it is not a particularly pleasant sight.

"That's enough, now, Walter. Do you promise to behave yourself from now on?"

"I promise, teacher," Walter says. Edwards turns his back and Walter slams his rolled-up newspaper over someone's head, as all the kids burst into song: "School days, school days, dear old golden rule days . . ."

Trains crossing and recrossing the country. Names of cities on station platforms. Walter in boardinghouse rooms practicing his dancing, studying routines from books. Postcards to his mother intercut with the rolled-up newspaper in the act, hitting the other kids over the head. Growing, until we see him at seventeen or so, tiptoeing through the sleeping car of a train late at night. The curtains to an upper berth open. A woman of at least thirty smiles at him, motions to him to join her.

Over a Chicago street, 1916, we hear an AGENT'S VOICE: "You're not bad, kid, but you're not so good either. I can get you a month on the Southern Wheel, or a week at the Chaney in Chicago."

"The *Chaney*!" Walter's voice says. "The Chaney's a toilet!"

"Yeah, but it's a toilet in Chicago. Whaddya want with your act, the Palace?"

"Listen, I can fool 'em, I swear to God."

"You can't fool the people, Walter. They know."

"Whadda they know? They know nothing."

"What'll it be, Walter? Chicago or the Cornpone Belt?"

We see the marquee of a rundown vaudeville house, the Chaney. Walter, in his late teens but dressed much older, approaches the theatre with a GIRL on his arm. She's very young, overdressed, wearing too much makeup; obviously a showgirl. A MAN ON A LADDER is putting the names of the acts on the marquee. Walter looks.

"Hey," Walter yells. "You spelled my name wrong. It's one 'l.'"

"You should inform your attorney," the man says, climbing down the ladder.

Walter looks again at the marquee.

"You know, I think I like it better that way."

"I'm so pleased," the man says. "Really I am."

Inside the box office of the Chaney. The MANAGER is sneaking a few bills from the cashbox into his pocket. He feels Walter's eyes on him, turns to see Walter watching, laughing.

A ghastly dressing room. Walter is searching wildly for the hole in the wall. He moves a picture, finds the hole, glues his eye to it. With his hands on his hips, he does an obscene little nautch dance as he peers into the next dressing room, where a couple of women are changing.

Onstage, finishing his act, feigning breathlessness, to very light applause. He thanks the audience loudly, but to himself he mutters, "You know-nothing bastards . . . you frigging cattle."

Hanging around backstage, nervous and predatory, he hears a couple yelling through one of the dressing-room doors. He puts his ear to the door. A HUSBAND AND WIFE TEAM are having a fierce argument.

"Don't lie to me," the husband is yelling. "I know where you were."

"Aw, you don't know nothing," the wife says.

"You were in the hotel with that greasy acrobat."

"He ain't so greasy," the woman says. "And if he is, I wish you had some of the same grease."

Walter is ecstatic.

"You dirty little tramp," the man says.

A loud slap is heard, followed by a high-pitched effeminate whimpering cry. As the door flies open, Walter steps back. The woman storms out. We see the husband, sitting at the dressing table with his head in his hands, crying.

"Just because I like it with a *man* once in a while, that don't make me no tramp!" the woman screams. Then she sees Walter.

"Hiya, Dora," he says, knowingly.

"Whadda *you* want?" she says. "What're you always hangin' around for? You're a goddamned nosy little bastard."

"Watch your language, honey," Walter says. "There's stage-hands present."

Another town. Walter finishes his act, muttering, "Applaud, applaud, you bastards."

The stage card is changed, announcing THE SINGING SANDERSONS, a family act: mother, father, teenage son, and daughter. Very wholesome, clean-cut. They come onstage singing "I'd Love to Live in Loveland with a Girl Like You."

Backstage. Leaving the theatre, Walter is stopped by the Sandersons.

"Walter, we're going over to the Trenton Grill to get a bite. Why don't you come with us?"

"Thanks, Agnes," Walter says. "I have a previous engagement." He winks at Mr. Sanderson.

"Are you sure, Walter?" he says. "Agnes is worried you spend too much time alone."

"Thanks, folks," Walter says. "Maybe tomorrow night."

Inside the Trenton Grill. We see the Sandersons eating dinner. It's warm and steamy inside. They seem completely happy, peacefully content with each other. Through the window, on the cold street, we see Walter watching them, hungry-looking and alone.

The agent's voice: "It's no good, kid. You're dying out there."

"I really had 'em," Walter's voice says.

"Yeah, and then you really lost 'em."

"I got pep. Everybody says so."

"Pep you got, but pep ain't talent. What you need is a partner. It's a shame you ain't sisters. Sister acts is good right now."

"What I need is something better than the second spot. I been a deuce so long, I'm starting to walk with a stoop. I'm sick of going on after the animal act. You ever tried dancing on elephant shit? It's not easy."

"I'm telling you, get yourself a partner. You tried sand-dancing, eccentric dancing, you even tried it on roller skates."

(Against this we see Walter: dancing while scattering sand from a straw hat; doing an awkward eccentric dance; waiting in the wings wearing roller skates, a look of pure hatred on his face as a CHIMPANZEE ACT finishes to great applause. As they come off, we see that the chimpanzees are all wearing roller skates.)

"Find yourself some cute kid. Maybe the audience will look at her."

We see a nice pair of legs moving backstage: RITA GREENE; followed by Walter's legs, pursuing her down the stage-door steps, out onto the street. The two pair of legs stop, go on, stop again. They move closer and closer, Walter's insinuatingly close to hers; we see them now onstage, dancing. Rita is dancing, Walter is standing to the side, pointing at her feet. The card reads WINCHELL AND GREENE.

A break:

"Say, darling," Walter is saying. "Do you know 'The Road to Mandalay'?"

"Yes," Rita says. "Would you like me to sing it?"

"No, I'd like you to take it."

In the audience, people are reading newspapers, sleeping, women are knitting, a fat man is picking his nose, etc. Someone laughs loudly, though; a desperate, lonely laugh.

"I knew you were out there," Walter says. "I just didn't know where you were sitting."

Rita sings a few bars of a current song.

"Her voice was trained," Walter says. "But it escaped and returned to the wilds."

"You stink," someone yells.

"Don't worry, folks, he's part of the act. Please, Dad . . ."

Rita twirls, stops. "What do you think of my execution?"

"I'm in favor of it," Walter says. Then, to the orchestra

leader: "Let's try and finish together tonight. I'm tired of win-
ning all the time."

The spotlight brings up the pale red of his rouged lips and
cheeks and the intense clear blue of his eyes. His face is
otherwise a powdered pallid green. He sings his song with a
terrible sincerity. There is something unsettling, almost sala-
cious, in the performance:

> *Amid fields of clover,*
> *'Twas just a little over,*
> *A hundred years ago.*
> *A handful of strangers,*
> *They faced many dangers,*
> *To make their country grow.*
> *It's now quite a nation,*
> *A land of inspiration,*
> *Where bells of Freedom ring.*
> *It's your land, it's my land,*
> *A great do-or-die land,*
> *Where everyone can sing.*

He removes his hat and steps to the footlights.

> *America, I love you.*
> *You're like a sweetheart of mine.*
> *From ocean to ocean,*
> *For you my devotion,*
> *Is touching each boundary line.*

> *Just like a little baby,*
> *Climbing his mother's knee,*
> *America, I love you,*
> *And there's a hundred million others like me . . .*

At the finish, Walter raises his straw hat and holds it so that the spotlight catches the red, white, and blue lining.

Very little applause.

In the wings, Walter stops Rita. "C'mon, let's grab another bow."

"What for, honey?"

"Yeah . . . You're right. Another minute of that, I'd have been asleep myself."

The next act hurries past them to the wings. "How were they?" he asks Walter.

"They loved *us*. You might find 'em a little tough."

In their dressing room, depressed. There is a telegram stuck in the mirror. Walter opens it.

"Never mind, sweetie," Rita is saying. "We'll get 'em in Atlanta."

Reading the telegram; "No, we won't. We've been canceled. The dirty rotten son-of-a-bitching bastard's canceled us. My God! What's in the grouchbag?"

Rita doesn't answer.

"Rita! Have we got enough dough to get back to New York?"

"Only for one," she says quietly.

A long freight train. A carload of chickens. Walter is scattering feed to them from a sack. His suit is filthy. On his face is a look beyond hatred and humiliation, as the noise of the chickens rises.

New York, late morning, in front of the Palace Theatre. A small group of second-string VAUDEVILLIANS is standing under the marquee.

"Brother, I've had it with that Coffee and Cake Time," one of them is saying. "They're too big to be small towns and too small to be big towns. I'd rather play in the sticks. They really appreciate my style there."

"That's because they're starved for anything that doesn't go moo or oink," Walter says, joining them. "Whaddya got, Morrie? You working?"

"Yeah," Morrie says. "I'm playing Dreamland in Coney."

"Dreamland? I thought they only did midget shows."

"They do. I give it some perspective," Morrie says. They all laugh. "It's only good showmanship."

"Midgets, feh," Walter says. "We were on the train with a midget act once. The one above me was the nervous type— all night long he paced up and down in his berth."

"It's a living," Morrie says.

"Back and forth, back and forth," Walter goes on, irritated at being interrupted.

"I got offered ten days at the Regal in Cincy," one of them says, "but I won't play that house. It's a jinx."

"Yeah . . . Albee wanted to put me on the Butterfield Circuit, but he wouldn't meet my price," another says.

"He didn't have change for a dollar," Walter says.

"You haven't got change for a match, so whaddya talking?"

"Listen, it's all for the birds," Walter says. "If you can't play here, why play at all?" (He indicates the Palace marquee.) "If you're not headlining, you might as well do what Ikey Bloom did, go into the fur business and make a living."

"The fur business ain't show business," one says.

"Show business!" Walter says. "I *hate* show business. You work like the goddamn milkman, you kill yourself, and for what? Chickenshit, and a bunch of goddamn lowbrow morons . . . people so dumb they'd rather spend Saturday night in some lousy firetrap than stay home and take a bath! That's what we get—that's what we play to—morons! I hate show business. You can take show business and stick it up George M. Cohan's flag-waving Jew-hating ass!"

"You can always come and work for me, Walter," IKEY BLOOM says, joining them. "With the mouth you got on you, you'd make a fortune. You work your own hours, you make twelve percent commission. You got the moxie. What do you say?"

"What!" Walter says. "And leave show business?"

A delicatessen on Broadway, early afternoon. Through the window, the bunch from the previous scene are on the sidewalk, saying good-bye to each other. Walter and Ikey Bloom remain at a large table. A waiter is cleaning up.

"So tell me, Ikey," Walter says. "How much money *are* you making?"

Ikey's eyebrows go up in mock surprise at Walter's nerve. "I'm making enough to buy you fellas a sandwich every time I find you out there. Shipwrecked on Hope Island."

"Don't mix me up with those guys," Walter says. "I'm going up. Another couple of months . . . Did you see *Variety*? They said we were sensational at the American Roof."

"I saw *Variety*," Ikey says. "They said you were 'pleasant.' "

"Well, I've got problems. Rita won't let me cut her specialty turn, and it just ain't hitting."

"Come on, Walter. We're old pals. Face it, it isn't going anywhere. Vaudeville's on its last legs. It's a tossup which is gonna go first, you or it."

"You mean to tell me you don't miss it?"

"Miss what? The applause? Listen, I had one week in 1914 when they had me headlining the Orpheum. I made eight hundred bucks that week. After ten years on the circuits. After that week, I was back to one fifty, the weeks I was working. Rachel was pregnant. I was never home. . . . You know."

"I know," Walter says. "That's the problem, Ikey. I know too much, but I don't know anything else. If I could take what I know and turn it into dough . . ."

"So, what do you know?" Ikey says.

"I know all the acts. I know who's stuck on who, who's in bed with who, who's mad at who, who's stealing whose material. I know who drinks too much, who doesn't drink enough, who gambles . . . I know everything about this business the public doesn't know."

"Tittle-tattle."

"No," Walter says. "Tittle-tattle's what you hear. I'm talking about what I *know.*"

"So you got a great line of shmooze. Who'll buy?"

"You call it shmooze, I say it's news."

"So go be a newspaperman."

"Oh boy. If only."

"What?" Ikey says. "You think it's above you? You ever *meet* a newspaperman? They make you guys look like the Prince of Wales. Come work for me, Walter, you'll really meet the big shots. I sold a coat to Ziegfeld this week. I know more headliners now than when I was on the stage."

"That's nice for you, Ikey," Walter says coolly.

"Okay, okay, I know. . . . You don't want to *meet* big shots. You want to *be* a big shot."

"How can you tell?" Walter says with fake coyness.

"How can I tell . . ." Ikey says.

We see Walter's hard, ravening grin, radiating all the hunger and ambition in the world.

.   .   .

First, we hear Winchell's voice, singing to himself, nasal and self-absorbed: "There's a broken heart for every light on Broadway . . ."

We hear the exaggerated sound of slow, one-finger typing. Walter and Rita, on a train, not speaking, sitting apart. We see them dancing onstage, simulating affection.

A crummy theatre in Scranton. Sound of typing continues, only slightly faster, as Walter sings to himself, "Yank my doodle, it's a dandy." Rita is alone in her dressing room; the camera moves to the open door of the manager's office. Walter, seated at a typewriter. We see him peck out the word NEWSSENSE.

A theatrical hotel in Moline. Rita, alone in bed. She turns out the light.

Behind the desk in the lobby, the sound of typing, faster. Walter singing, "By the sea, by the sea, by the C-U-N-T . . ." Under a naked lightbulb, he is typing.

We hear his voice now, speaking rapidly: "That was a great hand Freddie Conklin got the other night at the Grand in Scranton. By the way, Scranton's Freddie's hometown, and he comes from a *big* family . . ."

Theatre marquees, trains, etc. Walter scribbling notes on bits of paper, prowling backstage, moving around tables in theatrical restaurants.

Springfield, Mass., Walter typing in his dressing room. A couple of ACTORS look in on him.

"Oh, look," one says. "He's pretending to be a newspaperman. Isn't that adorable?"

"I remember when he was pretending to be a singer. I like this better."

"Frig yez," Walter says.

Rita sticks her head in. "Five minutes," she says.

"All right. All right," Walter says.

Walter's voice: "The Shuster Hotel in Hartford is a nicer place to stay since they fumigated the rooms . . . Dottie Davis isn't speaking to her manager, we hear. Whyzzat?"

Another theatre, backstage. Walter is seen taking a page out of a typewriter and walking briskly to the callboard, which only holds one or two items. With great purpose, like Luther nailing his petition to the church door, he ceremoniously tacks the page up.

His voice (against two tumblers onstage): "Which tumbler in the Carter Brothers act has tumbled hard for the waitress in Paul's Bar on Thirty-fourth Street? Is it the single one, or the one whose wife slaves over a hot stove in Queens? It's *both* of them."

We see a crowd, actors, clustered around the callboard, reading *Newssense*. One of them, an "electric" act, sticks a lightbulb in his mouth and it lights the board up. Walter is hanging around, watching them.

"Hey," the Manager says. "Who the hell said you could use my callboard?"

"What's it hurting you?" Walter says. "All you ever put up is some crummy notice telling us to turn the gas down when we leave our dressing rooms."

"Yeah," someone says. "Leave it alone."

"People spend a lot of dead time back here," Walter says. "This gives 'em something to do."

"Well," the Manager says. "I just like to be asked first." He starts reading it himself.

Typing sound, Walter singing, another theatre, another crowd around the callboard. Walter's voice:

"Seen outside a Cleveland movie house: Geraldine Farrar, supported for once by her husband." (A richly dressed middle-aged opera singer, drunk, being helped by her handsome young husband.) "Sorry to hear that Porkchops, the dog, is sick." (We see a sick dog.)

Walter standing by the crowd around the callboard. A BIG MAN, an acrobat, comes up to him and asks pleasantly, "Did you write this?"

"That's what it says," Walter says proudly.

"That's innaresting," the man says, and socks Walter hard.

Walter, with a black eye covered by pancake, comes offstage with Rita, arm in arm for the finish. The instant they're in the wings, they break apart from each other.

People crowded around the callboard. In the center of the group, dominating it, is a heavyset woman, SOPHIE TUCKER. In dress and bearing, she is obviously, blatantly different from these second-level actors. She radiates star power and confidence. Someone indicates Walter to her.

"Winchell?" she says.

"Miss Tucker," Walter says, awed.

"Kid," she says, "you got something here."

"Gee, you think so, Sophie?" he says, moving in fast.

"It's a shame to waste it on a callboard."

"What do you suggest?"

"You know Eddie Feldman at the *Vaudeville News?*"

"I know who he is."

"Go see him. Tomorrow. Tell him I sent you."

"I can use your *name?*"

"Absolutely, bubeleh. Use my name."

"I don't know what to say."

"Walter's at a loss for words," somebody cracks.

"How can I thank you?"

She eyes him shrewdly, warmly. "Don't worry about it, kid. Something'll come up." She moves away grandly. "So long, Show People," she says.

"Jeez," Walter says. "The bigger they are, the nicer they are."

"Is that why you're such a louse?" Rita says from the fringes of the group. She goes into the dressing room and closes the door.

La Hiff's Tavern, evening. An actor's restaurant. Walter slides into a booth beside JIMMY DEVANE, a vaudevillian.

"Jimmy, glad to see you," Walter says.

"Hiya, Walter. How's tricks?" He winks at the other people at his table.

"Great. Listen, Jimmy. I'm going over to the newspaper game." He's talking low and fast, so the others can't hear.

"Show business will never be the same," Devane says.

"And I'm selling the act. Six hundred. You interested?"

"Will it do for me what it's done for you?" Devane says, looking around at the rest of the party.

"All right, five hundred."

"Not if you throw in a hand-painted tie."

"C'mon, Jimmy, it's a good serviceable act. You could adapt it."

"Your act should remain an orphan. I'll give you seventy-five bucks for it. I can use it for scrap."

"You're nuts, seventy-five bucks."

"Freddie Castle only offered you fifty, so maybe I *am* nuts."

"All right, all right. Cash money." He gets up from the table.

"You a newspaperman now, Walter?" someone calls.

"Yeah. But don't tell my mudder. She thinks I'm playing piano in a whorehouse."

.   .   .

Late afternoon, in front of the Palace Theatre. More or less the same group of broken-down vaudevillians as before, standing around.

"Anybody got any dough? There's a game on in the Somerset," one of them says.

"Don't look at me," another says.

"Aw, he puts sawdust in his pockets so we won't hear the coins jingle."

"I couldn't *afford* sawdust," he says.

"Remember the Empire in Syracuse? Sweet little house. It's all moving pictures now. No acts."

"So get a job as an usher," one says. " 'He led her on and then he left her in the dark.' "

Walter, brisk and happy, snappily dressed, hurries by, carrying a press camera.

"Say, isn't that Valter Vinchell, the crackerjack young reporter for the *Vaudeville News?*"

"No. That's Valter Vinchell, the Albee pimp and union scab."

"Front-Page Farrel, the all-around schmerril."

"Hey, Walter. Take our picture."

"Waste of film," Walter says. "You're nice guys, but you're nobodies."

"Getting awfully upstage, aren't you, Walter?"

"All right, I'm sorry," Walter says. "You're *not* nice guys."

"How do you like working for the oppressor of the working stiff?"

"Yeah, Walter. You anti-union?"

"No," Walter says, over his shoulder. "I'm pro-Winchell."

Walter walks up the street, almost at a run. A MAN steps out of a restaurant as he passes.

"Hey, you! Winchell!"

"Whaddya want, Charlie? I'm in a hurry."

"What the hell kind of a deal you giving me? You sell me an ad in your rag, and then you write it in the paper that my blue-plate special's for the birds."

"You got a squawk, take it up with your cook. You buy an ad, you buy space in the paper, you don't buy me. I'm my own man."

He hurries on. A car pulls up in front of a theatre. Sophie Tucker steps out.

"Hey, Sophie!" Walter calls.

"Walter," she says.

"Hold it, doll," he says, taking her picture. "Thanks."

"Thank *you*, Walter," she says.

He scurries on.

We hear the voice of an OLD REPORTER, over shots of Winchell moving around town: talking to doormen, barbers, taxi drivers, showgirls; table-hopping; making frantic notes and jamming slips of paper into his bulging pockets.

The Old Reporter: "Be careful, don't ask too many questions. All you'll get is a reputation for asking too many questions. Pick it up on the q.t., a little here, a little there . . . and don't be afraid to go after the big shots. Remember, the bigger they are, the bigger the story. If you're writing about a woman, don't give her too many mentions in a row. Everybody'll think you're screwing her. . . ."

"And if I am?" Walter's voice says.

"It's up to you, Walter. You ask me for advice, this is what I got. And read the big guys. Read McIntyre. Read Adams. Read Damon Runyon."

"I hate sports," Walter's voice says.

"It isn't for the sports. It's for the writing."

．　．　．

We see DAMON RUNYON, still a young man, walking down the street, extremely dapper, self-contained, with a certain off-putting manner.

"Hey, Mr. Runyon," Walter calls, scampering after him.

"Yes?" Runyon says, eying him coolly.

"I'm Winchell."

"Yes?"

"*Vaudeville News*. Broadway columnist and advertising manager."

"Are you a columnist or an ad salesman?"

"I wear two hats," Walter says.

"Both of them old, I presume."

"You never saw my column?"

"Gossip is for women."

"Is that what you say?"

"Yep."

"Uh-huh. I thought maybe you could give me something on the fight."

"You can tell 'em Dempsey can't be stopped, unless it's by the Almighty Himself."

Walter jots this down, looks up to see Runyon has kept walking.

"Hey, thanks," he calls after him. "For nothing," he mutters to himself.

Runyon simply waves without looking back.

Walter stuffs the paper into a bulging pocket.

"Hey, Winchell," Runyon calls.

"Yeah?"

"You're ruining that suit."

．　．　．

Night; later the same night in 1943 as the opening scenes. We see Hedy Lamarr drift away from the car, through the door and into the lobby of the Waldorf-Astoria. Walter's car pulls away from the curb, and we hear Runyon talking.

"You still get your duds at the same place?"

"Yup," Walter says. "Nat Lewis. Two suits a year."

"Every year?"

"Every single year. How many suits you got?"

"Oh, Christ," Damon says. "I stopped counting when I hit a hundred. Where do you buy your shirts?"

"Woolworth's," Walter says. "You still wear your shirts once and throw them out?"

"I never did trust laundries. And I never found a woman who could iron."

"Maybe you've been looking in the wrong places," Walter says. "I'm going to Lindy's, see what the boys have for me."

"Deal me out," Damon says. "I'm bushed."

"I'm just getting started."

A Broadway record store. Walter is inside a listening booth, alone, dancing happily to Ethel Smith's recording of "Tico-Tico." We hear the voice of a PRESS AGENT:

"Never met Walter Winchell. Do it all over the phone. If you meet him, he'll know what you look like, and that's where your heartaches begin."

Lindy's restaurant, late night. We see the Press Agent sitting with a bunch of fellow P.A.s, talking to a young member of their group.

"How so?" the YOUNG P.A. says.

"Because he hates everybody with a face," one of them says, the SOUR P.A.

"You give him a bad item," the First P.A. goes on, "you do your time like everybody else. Feed him some fat, and you're back in again. If he knows you, if you think you're his friend, he'll take it out in flesh."

"Unless you want to wax his car or clean his shoes," the Sour P.A. says.

"I can see you don't believe me. You think you're so charming, it'll be different with you."

"Naw, I believe you," the Young P.A. says, with no conviction whatsoever.

"Jeez," another P.A. says, "did you see the column this morning? Bette Davis has cancer."

"She better have cancer, or she's in big trouble."

"Walter Winchell, Walter Winchell, big frigging deal, Walter Winchell," the Sour P.A. says.

"He *is* a big frigging deal," the First P.A. says. "He gets a hundred grand a year for his column, and he don't even write it."

"Go on," the Young P.A. says.

"We damn near write it for him," one says. "Without us, there wouldn't *be* any Walter Winchell."

"He couldn't write a whole column himself if his life depended on it."

"He couldn't write a whole sentence," the Sour P.A. says. "*Flash!* Dot . . . dot . . . dot . . . Walter Winchell is an illiterate cocksucker."

"I'll tell him you were saying so," the First P.A. says.

"Ya would, ya treacherous bastard you. Go ahead. I can make a living without Walter Winchell."

"Listen," one of them says, "he admits it. He *says* he's a shitheel."

"He *better* admit it. And it isn't just his heel."

"Aw, he's not so bad once you get to know his income."

One of the P.A.s turns his eyes up to the ceiling and folds his hands in prayer. "Walter . . . I'm not even listening!"

"Shit, here he comes."

Walter rushes into Lindy's, waving, taking greetings. Big buzz in the room. The P.A.s fall all over themselves getting to their feet, greeting him effusively. The Sour P.A. is of course the most obsequious.

"Walter," he says. "That was a *hell* of a broadcast last Sunday. Maybe the best you ever did."

"Thanks, Mickey," Walter says, barely looking at him. They start to produce envelopes and folded bits of paper. One of them very cautiously extends a page toward Walter, but he's stopped with a cold glare.

"Put it in the want ads, Shepsie," Walter says. With all the paper clutched in his hand, he moves to a corner table, waving to people as he goes. His cheesecake and coffee are already there.

"What the hell did you do?" one of them asks Shepsie.

"I saw him getting off the elevator in the St. Moritz with Whitey Franklin's wife the other day. While Whitey was in the hospital with gallstones."

"That's it?" the Young P.A. says.

"That's it," Shepsie says. "You still wanna meet Walter Winchell, kid?"

Predawn, Central Park Zoo. Walter is tossing peanuts through the bars of the monkey cage. He is attended by a few of the Press Agents from Lindy's. Among them is the Young P.A. Out of Walter's hearing, one of them turns to another.

"What a life this is," he says. "We feed the Lion, and the Lion feeds the monkeys."

.   .   .

Dawn. The City Room of the New York *Daily Mirror*. Walter breezes in carrying a briefcase, some envelopes under his arm. Various REPORTERS and EDITORS greet him.

"Hello, Big Man . . . Morning, King . . . Hiya, Walter."

"Greetings, Gates, what percolates?"

"It's all there on your desk, God."

He goes into his office, closes the door, locks it.

On the wall is a huge map of the United States, with something like a thousand American flags stuck across it: a flag for every paper that carries his column.

He tears envelopes open, arranges scraps over his desk, begins typing, singing to himself: "We'll have a blue room, a new room, a Jew room, Where two can live as cheap as one, Providing one drops dead . . ."

He is terribly animated, charged with physical energy, as though this very activity has galvanized him. We realize that he is more truly alive doing this than at any other time. We see the head on the paper in his typewriter: *Things I Never Knew Till Now*.

As he works, over the sound of his typing, we hear the voice of EMILE GAUVREAU, cultivated, humorous, somewhat pompous:

"And in the corner sat a figure of deceptive humility, white-faced and ravenous, looking up occasionally, startled. He pecked a typewriter nervously, with a frenzied determination."

As Gauvreau speaks, we see Times Square, circa 1925; the door to the offices of the New York *Graphic*; into Walter's office. On the door is written DRAMA EDITOR. Walter is typing, in the manner described by Gauvreau's v.o. In his typewriter, we read *Your Broadway and Mine*. A man sticks his head in the door.

"Gauvreau wants to see you."

"What the hell does he want?"

"I believe he wants to kill you."

Walter walks through the City Room. We see a photograph, prominently displayed, of the publisher, BERNARR MACFADDEN, dressed only in a loincloth, muscles rippling. A man is hanging from a steampipe on the ceiling by his long black hair.

"Jesus," Walter mutters. "What the hell is this?"

"Friend of the boss's," someone says. "Says he's got the strongest hair in the world."

Walter enters Gauvreau's office. Their mutual antagonism is immediately obvious.

"Whaddya want?" Walter demands.

Gauvreau moves with a limp around his desk.

"Mr. Winchell, our publisher has certain interests and biases which you may find peculiar, but he happens to own this newspaper. Make fun of him in your free time . . ."

"What free time?"

". . . but not in your column."

"I don't know what you're talking about."

Gauvreau reads: "Bernarr Macfadden asks, What could be more pleasant than a cold bath before breakfast? Answer: No cold bath before breakfast."

Walter laughs, turns to leave.

"I'm not finished, Winchell. You say here that Herbert Stanwyck is about to leave his wife for an ingénue."

"Correct-o."

"Has his wife filed for divorce?"

"No . . ."

"Then this isn't news," Gauvreau says, striking out the lines with a blue pencil.

"But it's true," Walter says.

"This McCambridge woman . . . You refer to her as an

'heiress.' To what is she an heiress? . . . Is she in fact an heiress at all? . . . Will you define heiress?"

"An heiress is any woman who can pay her own hotel bill."

Gauvreau runs his pencil through this, reads: "A blondiful sextress is asking for trouble fooling around with married men. Are there any other kind? Heh heh heh."

Walter joins in on the last two lines, obviously in love with his style.

"What's wrong with that?"

"It isn't English! That's what's wrong."

"Yeah? And this ain't the *New York Times*," Walter says. "This is barely a real newspaper. Look."

He grabs a copy of the *Graphic* from the desk. We see the headline: MY FRIENDS DRAGGED ME INTO THE GUTTER; the sub-head: AND WILD HORSES COULDN'T DRAG ME BACK. We see the "cosmograph," a faked composite photo depicting Enrico Caruso and Rudolph Valentino in heaven.

"If God wanted something to wipe his fanny with, he'd reach down and use this. The *Graphic*: for fornication and against vaccination. And most of the people who buy it only buy it to read me."

"A man who can't read," Gauvreau says.

"And the boss'll back me up. You know he will. Must run, Gauvreau. Toodle-oo." He leaves. In the City Room, he passes Bernarr Macfadden, a man in his sixties, of almost supernatural good health, abundant white hair, glowing red cheeks, etc.

"Hello, *Bernarr*," Walter says, blatantly making fun of the name.

"Morning, Walter," Macfadden says.

"How are you feeling? You look a little pale," Walter says, leaving the City Room.

Macfadden goes into Gauvreau's office.

"Only a paper like the *Graphic* could have spawned a reptile like that," Gauvreau says.

"Never mind, Emile. Remember, he's out there all the time. He has the energy of ten men. He knows everybody. I'm not sure what a Broadway column really is, but he certainly keeps the city desk informed."

"He's such a vulgar little man."

"And ours is such a vulgar little paper. Anyway, I rather like him, don't you?"

"No. I despise him."

"Harness him, then," Macfadden says.

Walter, alone at a table in Dave's Blue Room. He picks up on a couple behind him, who are laughing heartily at something the man has said.

He bolts over to the table.

"Hi!" he says.

"Hi!" the man says, in a sarcastic and very unfriendly imitation of Walter.

"What's the gag?" Walter says.

"What's it to you?" the man says.

"If it's any good, I'll put it in my column."

"Now that's a big frigging deal."

"Some people think so," Walter says.

"Say, who the hell *are* you?" the man says. "We're dining, do you mind?"

"Not at all," Walter says, suddenly turning to the woman. There is something terrible in the force of his attention that completely wipes the smile off her face.

"Mrs. Fletcher . . ." Walter says, "please resume dining . . . and laughing."

Over footage of Times Square, Broadway, we hear Walter's

voice: "That was Mrs. Howard Fletcher head to head in Dave's Blue Room the other eve, but her partner in oh so intimate hilarity wasn't Mr. Fletcher . . . And so with a heavy heart to my Broadway, where I upstaged all whom I encountered . . ."

The Broadway footage ends, the lights vanish.

Walter is walking down a dimly lighted apartment hallway. Over this, we hear Walter's voice, reciting a poem from his column:

> *Every morn I ramble on you*
> *While the incandescents sleep.*
> *With my troubles I come to you,*
> *For I'm one of your black sheep.*

He stops, knocks on a door. No reply. He knocks again, harder. A baby starts crying. We hear a woman's voice: JUNE.

"Who is it?"

"Walter Winchell."

"What do you want?"

"I hear you're minding a baby for someone. I thought it'd make a cute item for my column."

"No thanks, we don't want any."

"Taffy Stryker sent me."

"You're a friend of Taffy's?"

"We're like this," Walter says, crossing his fingers.

"Like what?"

"Open the door."

The door opens a little. Walter holds up his crossed fingers. "Like this."

June opens the door. She's an attractive woman of around twenty-five. Walter begins looking her up and down. She's unfazed by this, amused.

"So tell me, whose baby is it?"

"A friend's."

"Must be a very good friend," Walter says.

"*Very* good," June says. "Why, do you think it's mine?"

"Well . . ."

"You know, maybe it is. Maybe I gave birth between Boston and New Haven. I was so tired I really don't remember."

"You know, it wouldn't hurt you to be nice to me."

"I know all about being nice to you. I can make it on my feet or I can make it on my back, and either way you're a good guy to know. In fact, Mr. Winchell . . ."

"Call me Walter."

"When I know you better . . . In fact, Mr. Winchell, I'm not planning to make it either way. I'm out of the show. I wasn't canned, I left."

"I'm still a good guy to know."

"There are people who would give you an argument there. You're sort of cute. You might even be a nice guy, if you didn't act like such a big shot."

"But, baby, everybody loves a big shot."

"Everybody loves a *real* big shot. Someday, with a little luck, you could become as big as your mouth."

She closes the door softly.

For a split second Walter's at a loss. "Hey!" he calls. "You gotta get to know me. My mother wouldn't let me in the house until I was fourteen years old."

Walter and June are finishing lunch in Billy La Hiff's.

"I was on that wheel as long as you were," June is saying. "You may be impressed by all that baloney, but not me. I like to go to bed early."

Walter looks at his watch. "Is two-thirty too early?"

"No kidding. As far as I'm concerned, Broadway is just a great big waste of electricity."

"But, baby, it's my life. And my living. Can't I have you *and* Broadway?"

"I think you can have anything you want in this life. But anyway, you're a married man."

"Not anymore I'm not," Walter says. "I had that contract canceled."

"Really?"

"Really."

June looks at him. "In that case, you can kiss me if you like."

"Listen, Junie," Walter says fervently, "I got a certain rep . . . Everybody on the street knows I'm no damn good, but they sort of like me anyway."

"I sort of like you," June says.

"Do you like me, or are you just getting used to me?"

"I must like you," June says, "because I'll never get used to you."

The West Forties, late afternoon. A group of CHORUS GIRLS in costume is seated on the steps of a brownstone across the street from a theatre. One of them is reading the *Graphic*, the rest are playing jacks.

"Winchell says you sleep on your left side and hate carrots," Chorine One says.

"I wonder how he found out about the carrots," Chorine Two says.

Walter and June, arm in arm, pass the theatre across from the chorus girls.

"There he is," Chorine One says.

"Hello, Walter," Chorine Two calls.

June gives Walter a tough, amused look.

"Hi, girls," Walter says, waving.

"Hey, watch it," one of the girls says to Chorine Two. "That's his wife."

"His wife?" Chorine Two says. "Poor her."

Late afternoon (continued). Walter and June walking past a bunch of college men, who sing as they go down the street, "Hail, hail, the gang's all here, What the heck do we care, What the heck do we care . . ."

In front of Billy La Hiff's Tavern, West Forty-seventh Street. Billy is in the doorway.

They greet each other warmly.

"Go ahead up, honey," Walter says. "I'm going into the mines. Anybody in there?"

"The usual bums," Billy says.

Inside Billy La Hiff's. Walter moves around the room like a cat. He spots RUNYON alone at a corner table, reading a newspaper. He slips around behind him, sees that he's reading Winchell's column.

"Gossip's for women, huh? Well, kiss me in the dark."

Runyon looks up, expressionless, then smiles. "Waldo Winchester. Have a drink."

"Naw, let me get you one. What're you drinking?"

"I'm not drinking drink anymore. I'll have a—Oh, Christ, what does it matter?—a sarsaparilla, a ginger ale, a cup of coffee . . ."

"Well, what do you think?" Walter says, indicating the column.

"It's the best thing in the paper," Runyon says caustically, then laughs. "I like it. Everybody likes it."

"I know," Walter says. "It's all anybody's talking about. When I think of all the years I spent on the wrong streetcar, I could cry."

"You weren't wasting your time," Runyon says. "You could never have gotten away with this ten years ago. Before the war, you would have starved."

"It's the times," Walter says. "Gene Fowler says it's the two hundredth anniversary of the cuckoo clock. Al Capone's as famous as Al Jolson."

"Worth more, too."

"It's all going nuts, and it's all going into the papers. You watch, this is just the beginning for me."

"Your modesty's too becoming."

"What have I got to be modest about?"

"And I admire your self-confidence. On the other hand, there's a saying where I come from."

"How does it go? I'll put it in my column."

"It goes, 'Meat's not meat till it's in the pan.' "

THE RISE OF WALTER WINCHELL

This is essentially a montage sequence, with the odd break for dialogue. It could be played against the driving, escalating rhythms of Glenn Gray's "Casa Loma Stomp," almost choreographed to it, like elements in a musical number, showing:

WW front row and backstage on Broadway.

The Algonquin Hotel; the Round Table; WW and the cognoscenti: Woollcott, Parker, Benchley, Mencken.

Typing madly in his office: Scraps from the column are seen, emphasizing WW's "slanguage." Renovating, phffft, straining at the leash, cinemagic, that way, *etc. Column titles: Pillar of Gab, Memos of a Midnighter, Stardust Street, New York Novelette. Orchids. Scallions.*

WW and Gauvreau quarreling. Gauvreau throws a bust of Napoleon at him, missing him. Walter thumbs his nose.

Lunch with Macfadden, who eats a pile of greens garnished with nuts, while Walter wolfs down a steak.

Strolling with June. The camera pulls back: we see that Walter is pushing a baby carriage, smiling proudly.

Club Intime (Texas Guinan), the Onyx Club, the Hyena Club, the Drool Inn, the Cotton Club. Speakeasies. Sometimes with June, more often alone.

Headlines: HARDING IS DEAD; HALL-MILLS MURDER VERDICT: GUILTY; LINDY LANDS; GANG WARFARE ERUPTS!

Two cars speeding down the street at night, exchanging machine-gun fire.

Club Intime, night. Walter is on the dance floor with a pretty girl. Two men move through the dancers. One of them taps Walter on the shoulder, grabs his arm, and pulls him back from the girl, while the other moves in to take his place with her. They're both very tough guys. The one who has taken Walter's place dances much better than he does. He holds the girl tight and stares into her eyes, smiling at her. She's both frightened and excited. She relaxes, and smiles back at him.

The other hood moves Walter through the club with great force, up to a table in the back, where a small, powerfully built, expensively dressed man is sitting alone: OWNEY MADDEN.

"Siddown, kid," Owney says to Walter.

"Hiya, Owney," Walter says nervously.

"Do I know you?" Madden says.

"I know you, Owney," Walter says.

"But you and me haven't been introduced?"

"No."

"Then what the fuck has *my* name been doing in *your* mouth all over town?"

"Aw, everyone knows you, Owney. They call you the second mayor of New York."

"Yes, but I don't ask them to. In some rackets, the best publicity is no publicity. You wanna plug my joints, be my guest. But leave my name out. Completely out. You understand what I'm telling you?"

"Sure," Walter says. "But I could still help you out."

Madden's pleasant, almost friendly manner changes in a flash. "How in hell could a little punk like you help a guy like me?" he snarls.

"Well," Walter says, "I happen to know that tootsie you've been running around with did time on a fraud rap a couple of years ago. Every time you go out with her, you're violating your parole . . . Just in case somebody wanted to make something out of it."

Owney looks nonplused. "How come nobody told me this?"

"Probably because nobody knew it."

"Maybe some people ain't nosy enough," Madden says thoughtfully.

Walter laughs. "Being nosy gets a bad rap. Personally, I like to know what's going on. They say knowledge is power. You ever heard that one, Owney?"

"I heard something like it," Owney says.

Headlines: LITTLE BOY PEEP; THE PRINCE OF PEP; BROADWAY IS GOLD-PAVED FOR WALTER WINCHELL.

Winchell is stopped going into the Shubert Theatre. Column item: "A certain reporter has been barred from all Shubert openings. Now he can wait three nights, and go to the clos-

ings." Sneaking into the Shubert backstage with the Marx Brothers, dressed as Harpo.

Walter more pursued than pursuing in the gathering of items.

WW coming home at dawn, tiptoeing into the baby's room for a kiss. June is just waking up.

Proceeding from Texas Guinan, a series of introductions to famous and powerful people, until it is clear that WW is one of them.

Buying the boys from in front of the Palace a sandwich, grabbing the check from Ikey Bloom.

Ringside with Runyon, as Dempsey is knocked through the ropes, almost into their laps.

Polly Adler's brothel.

Waiters carrying trays of drinks, Charlestoning. WW dancing all night in various clubs, with various women.

Culminating in the Earl Carroll "orgy": a wild party where the guests fill their glasses from a bathtub full of champagne; in the bathtub is a naked, laughing woman.

A corridor, the New York *Graphic*. ED SULLIVAN, an athletic-looking man in his mid-twenties, is approaching the elevator. Walter scurries after him.

"Sullivan!" Walter calls. "Hey, Ed, wait a sec. I gotta talk to you."

"What's the matter?" Sullivan says.

"Listen, Ed, do me a favor, will you? Jimmy Walker says Hearst is gonna offer me a job on the *Mirror*. It's a hell of a break for me. You and the Chief are pretty close . . . I was wondering if you'd talk to him . . . Sort of feel him out . . . I gotta get out of this contract."

"Yeah, maybe," Sullivan says. "We're going fishing this weekend."

"Aw, great, Ed, great. But for Christ sake, don't let Gauvreau find out that you went behind his back."

"Listen, don't *you* let Gauvreau find out about it. That's all I need. He's a touchy little son of a gun."

"That's because he's a physical and mental cripple," Walter says. The elevator doors close. "Fishing," Walter says. "Yecch."

We see the closed door of Gauvreau's office. We can hear him shouting inside.

We see Gauvreau, browbeating a humiliated Ed Sullivan.

"In future, if you have a future, just remember who the editor of this paper is. Understand?"

"Yeah, yeah, I understand," Sullivan says. "There's just one thing. How did you find out that I talked to the Chief about Winchell?"

"How do you *think* I found out?" Gauvreau says, smirking. "Winchell told me."

We see the door to Gauvreau's office flung open. Sullivan charges out, enraged.

"Where is he?" he yells, looking around. "Where is the son-of-a-bitch?"

Dave's Blue Room. Walter, sitting with a few people, is about to attack a huge piece of chocolate cake when Sullivan rushes in, grabs him by the tie and pulls him halfway across the table. Walter's face is covered in icing.

"I swear to God, Ed, he forced it outta me!"

"I ought to drag you into the can and put your head in the toilet where it belongs," Sullivan says. "If you ever speak to me again, that's what you'll get." He shoves Walter back into his seat.

Bernarr Macfadden's bedroom, 3:30 in the morning. Macfadden is sleeping. The phone rings.

"Hello?" he says.

"Damn it, Bernarr," Walter shouts into the phone, "you're standing in the way of my career!"

"Walter?" Macfadden says.

"I want my freedom! Listen, Bernarr . . . I saw you."

"What did you see, Walter?" Macfadden says pleasantly.

"I saw you in Dinty Moore's. You were eating a big fat raw steak. The blood was running down your chin."

"Now, Walter, we both know that's not true."

"Yeah, but we're the only ones who do. I'll tell them all what a phony you are."

"Would you really do that?"

"Whatever I have to do. Let me go, Bernarr. Today! Before I kill that one-legged schoolteacher . . ."

"Emile has both his legs, Walter. One of them is just a little . . ."

"Today!" He slams down the phone.

Gauvreau's office. Gauvreau is seated, talking to Walter. As he talks, he toys with a piece of paper: Walter's release from the *Graphic*.

"We were never up to much here, but somehow this became a much lower newspaper than even we intended." He hands Walter the release. "I think we have you to thank for that."

"It was my pleasure," Walter says.

"You're a terrible price to pay for freedom of the press," Gauvreau says.

Walter grabs the paper, rubbing it lovingly against his chest. "Goodbye, Emile, and drop dead."

Walter breaks into a maniacal tap dance, waving the paper, dancing out of Gauvreau's office across the small City Room, past several reporters, and straight out the door.

FIRST REPORTER (looking at the empty doorway): "Goodbye, Walter."

SECOND REPORTER: "It's been great working with you all these years. . . . Say, Walter, how many years has it been?"

THIRD REPORTER: "And all the help we gave you . . . Don't mention it. We were happy to do it."

FIRST REPORTER: "Good luck, Walter. You've got a lot coming to you."

We see the front page of the New York *Mirror,* Walter's picture, the banner lead, KING OF BROADWAY.

We see the word *Broadway* repeated: in type, in neon, painted on tavern windows, on a street sign. We see the door to Walter's new office, the map of the United States on the wall as the little flags begin to appear, heralding the rise of Winchell's syndication, as Walter sings: "Don't bring a frown to old Broadway . . . Say, you've got to clown on Broadway . . . Your troubles here, they're out of style . . . cause Broadway always wears a smile . . ." and we see:

1931

Walter, walking-dancing down Broadway, past a blind man with his hat on the sidewalk, whistling "I'll See You in My Dreams." Walter sings a few phrases as he passes, but doesn't drop anything in the hat. He spots HELLINGER and JOLSON coming out of a club.

"Hey, Marcus, good to see you," Winchell says. "You doing yourself any good?"

"Breaking even," Hellinger says.

"Jolie," Walter says, "how's your Yiddishe Mammy?"

"Eating every day," Jolson says.

"How was California?" Walter asks Hellinger.

"Like a bad dream, except you get paid for it," Hellinger says. "How's June?"

"Out to here," Walter says, holding his hands in front of his stomach.

"You dirty dog you," Jolson says.

"Look who's talking."

"You're looking flush," Hellinger says.

"I'm loaded," Walter says.

And as he says this, a SHABBY MAN in the crowd snaps to attention and focuses on them. He's been in the background all along. He's pathetically dressed, almost in rags, but bright looking, too bright; crazy, in fact. Unobserved by the three, he begins following them, absorbed in their conversation.

"If I go for this broadcast deal, I'll be taking four grand a week, and that's just the on-top money," Walter says. "That's seven, eight grand a week."

"You'll never make it in radio," Jolson says. "You talk too fast."

"You, shmuckelheimer," Walter says. "You coulda had half *The Jazz Singer,* and you took it in salary. I thought Jews were supposed to be smart."

Jolson laughs. "Yeah, but what a salary."

"I know what those momsers paid you, Jolie. Half a million."

Hearing these figures the Shabby Man puts his hands on

his cheeks and rocks his head from side to side, rolls his eyes, lifts his eyebrows, still unseen by the three.

"Listen," Hellinger says, "as long as you're happy."

"What's happy? Who's happy?" Walter says. "There's always more. And there's always some hungry kid coming up behind you."

"The old story," the Shabby Man says.

They look at him, and then ignore him.

"You know," Walter says, "Runyon made four hundred grand last year."

"And we all know how happy *he* is," Hellinger says.

"Mark's from a rich family, so he doesn't like to talk about dough," Walter says. "Except to say, 'Can you lend me a few hundred dollars.' "

"Which reminds me," Hellinger says. "I'll drop it by your office in the morning."

"He'll borrow it from me," Jolson says.

"I beg your pardon," the Shabby Man says. "But does anybody here need any money?"

"For Christ's sake," Walter says to the man. "Go get your watch oiled, why don't you? The goddamn *bums* around here . . ."

"I'm not a bum," the Shabby Man says indignantly.

"What the hell are you then?" Walter says.

"I'm a vagabond!"

Walter, Hellinger, and Jolson walk down the street laughing.

Late that night, the sidewalk in front of The Stork Club. There is a small crowd of people standing around on the street, peering in through the closed doors. Walter comes up quickly, cutting through them like a knife.

"You better have a reservation," somebody says.

"Hey, you're Walter Winchell!" another says.

"No fooling," Walter says.

"That's Winchell. He doesn't need a reservation."

Walter goes inside, to the entrance of the club's main room. A velvet rope is stretched across the entranceway, one end attached to the Reservations Captain's station.

"Can I help you?" the Captain asks arrogantly.

"Yes, you can. You can move this frigging rope at once and let me pass."

"Have you reserved with us?"

"Where's Billingsley?"

"What name shall I say?"

"Winchell," Walter says loudly. He has been playing contemptuously with the rope. Now he tugs it angrily.

Billingsley, who has been standing nearby, turns sharply at the sound of the name. He walks quickly over, releases the rope, puts an arm around Walter, and smacks the Captain in the back of the head, all in one fluent purposeful movement. He smiles his cold smile as he walks Walter into the room.

"I hope you'll be happier at your next job," Walter sneers at the Captain.

"I hired him as a favor to a friend," Billingsley says.

"Jewish friend or Italian friend?" Walter says.

"I can't remember. I have so many friends."

Seated with Billingsley, Walter looks around the room. It is the embryo of The Stork Club of the opening scene, and it is at least half empty. A pianist is playing "Stardust."

"Texas told me to give your joint a play," Walter says.

"That was nice of her," Billingsley says. "That broad sure has a big mouth."

"She sure has." Walter looks around. "You're half empty and you've got the rope up. There's customers out on the street."

"They don't know it's half empty."

"Money is money," Walter says.

"The world is full of drinkers who'll spend money in your joint if they think they can have a slice of your ass. This isn't a saloon. And besides, tomorrow morning, all those people out there will tell their friends that they went to The Stork Club last night and couldn't get in. Let 'em go to Schrafft's."

"See what you mean."

"Makes the people inside feel better, too."

"I feel better already," Walter says. "Isn't that Myrna Loy?"

"Yep. I get a lot of that type. I spent a bundle on the lights. You set 'em up right, they make a plain dame look beautiful, and a beautiful dame look like a goddess. Everybody sees what they want to see. Even sober."

"How come you call it The Stork Club?"

Billingsley shrugs. "Why not?"

"I mean, where'd it come from?"

"I haven't the faintest idea."

"Cute name. Better than the Shmegegge Club. Shall I give it a mention in my column?"

"It's your column."

"Good booze, too," Walter says, tasting his drink. "Where'd you get it?"

Billingsley smiles his secret smile. "I'm the smart little feller who stocked up his cellar."

STARDUST

We see the Winchell column, the word *orchids* . . . "Sherman Billingsley's Stork Club, the New Yorkiest place in New York . . ."

We see the club in successive shots, with bigger crowds on

the street, more glamorous crowds inside. The velvet rope goes up and down. The pianist from the previous scene is now part of a trio, playing "Stardust." At the end of the sequence, he is the leader of a small orchestra, and The Stork Club is an institution.

We see Walter entering the club with some people. He stops, points admiringly at Billingsley's necktie.

Walter, in his office at the *Mirror*, receives a parcel. Opening it, we see a dozen neckties identical to Billingsley's.

Walter, entering The Stork Club men's room, passes a woman who is coming out.

"Hiya, Peggy," he says.

"Hiya, Walter," she says. She drops a coin into the attendant's plate. He is the former Reservations Captain.

Walter and June step into the lobby of The Stork Club. Walter spots a nervous press agent, WOLFIE, skulking around by the hat-check counter.

"Hiya, Walter," Wolfie says, tentative and frightened. He tries to avoid looking at June, whose presence is clearly making this even more humiliating for him.

"Well well well," Walter says. "If it isn't the Wolf Man. I'm surprised at you, Wolfie, showing your fat face around here."

June gives Walter a reproachful look, but he doesn't catch it.

"Listen, Walter, I can explain . . . I'm really sorry," Wolfie says.

"Oh *ho*, I'll bet you're sorry."

"I thought it was the McCoy."

"Anybody in your business who falls for a fakola like that

hadn't ought to be in your business," Walter says. "Which you won't be for long when your clients find out that you're dead as far as Winchell is concerned."

"Please, Walter, let me make it up to you."

June's embarrassment is visibly increased by this.

"How can you make it up to me?" Walter says. "You're dead. Now go get yourself buried before I call the Board of Health."

He walks away from Wolfie.

"Okay, okay," Wolfie calls, desperate. "I *admit* it was a fake. . . . But it was *exclusive!*"

Walter stops, laughs at this; Wolfie's chutzpah has reached him.

"All right, all right," he says. "Consider yourself resurrected."

June's relief seems greater even than Wolfie's.

"You won't be sorry, Walter," Wolfie calls.

"Sure, sure," Walter says, walking on with June. "Another minute of that, he'd have gone into the Weep . . . 'My kid needs new shoes . . . my mudder's got a hoinia . . . the Hotsy-Totsy Club's gonna can me . . .' Press agents, what a bunch of lowlifes . . ."

The Stork Club. Walter is with June. Billingsley greets her with what passes as warmth, kissing her on the cheek.

"This is a rare pleasure," he says. "This must be family night. Damon and Patrice just came in."

We see Runyon with his wife, PATRICE, a tall striking redhead. Walter and June greet them as they pass their table. Patrice seems to have eyes for everyone in the room but Damon.

Seated at their table, Walter says, "All right, honey? Smoke bother you?"

"No, it's fine."

"You let me know, and we'll blow."

We see Damon and Patrice from June's p.o.v. "God, look at those two," she says. "They look like strangers."

"Well, you can't always tell by appearances," Walter says. "For instance, look at those two over there."

We see an attractive young couple, holding hands and gazing passionately at each other.

"Crazy about each other, right?" Walter says. "They're getting married next week. Now look over there, two tables away."

We see another couple. The man is quite handsome.

"That's the guy she's *really* in love with. She's with him any time she can sneak away. She just can't help it . . . Now that guy over there, with the brunette . . . she's not his wife. She's a paid escort."

"A whore, you mean," June says.

"A rose by any other name, but very high-class. His wife is in a hotel over on Forty-sixth Street with the guy she's really mad about. Now those two . . ."

We see another couple sitting together.

"They're both making a play for the same girl, a dancer in the Earl Carroll show. And her, see her . . ."

We see a beautiful blonde girl on the dance floor.

"She's got six guys on the string. They're all paying for her singing lessons. So she'll be in here tomorrow night but he won't. Every night, Monday through Saturday, she's in here with a different guy."

"And Sunday?" June says.

"Sunday she visits her mother. And if you told any of them what's really going on, they'd never speak to you again."

"You *know* all these people?" June says.

"Them, and plenty more."

"My God. If you dropped dead tomorrow, I wouldn't know a single person at the funeral."

"Don't say 'funeral,' " Walter says.

"But don't they love each other a little?" June says.

"Who knows? Personally, I think it's all for show."

"But for whose benefit?"

Walter looks surprised. "For whose benefit? For *my* benefit."

June looks terribly hurt, almost frightened, as though she is seeing clearly and for the first time what Walter really does, and who he is. "Nice friends you've got."

"Aw, honey, they're not my friends. I don't *have* friends. You know, if I let people get too close, I couldn't write about them."

"Does that go for me and the kids, too?" June says.

We see a girl trio around a microphone in a radio studio. One of them takes a wad of chewing gum out of her mouth, sticks it behind her ear, and they start singing the current novelty hit "Mrs. Winchell's Little Boy."

Against this, we see *Time* magazine, with a painting of Walter on the cover; we see the article inside, with pictures of Walter at work, with his family, etc. A voice reads an extract from the piece: "He stays up all night, and from sundown until dawn he may visit a dozen places . . . He has been called bad names: Scandalmonger, Little Boy Peep, The Man at the Keyhole . . ."

This fades into a shot of *Vanity Fair*, a caricature of Winchell, and the prim, cultured voice of Alexander Woollcott: "Softshoeing into a dreary phase of American journalism came Master Winchell, his eyes wide with the childlike interest all newcomers have, his nervous staccato pace as characteristic of his day as the rhythms of George Gershwin. Perhaps it is true that he is lacking in taste, but he has a far more valuable asset. For want of a better term, let us call it *zest!*"

We see the girls again, finishing the song. They stand away

from the microphone, and we see Walter looming up over it, powerfully, epically. He grabs it, pushes his hat back on his head, and lets go with:

"Okaaayyy America! This is Walter Winchell, your Broadway Newsboy, with all the news you'll never read in the *New York Times*.

"Item: We hear that the recent Barrymore-Selznick brawl started over a crack about the Hebrews . . .

"Item: Kitty Roy, who isn't a blonde anymore, and Pancho, the bandleader, gave each other a piece of their alleged minds in the Mayfair lobby at three-forty-five yesteryawning . . . Some fun, eh, Kit?

"Item: Peggy Entwhistle jumped to her death in Hollywood because the famed director who wooed her produced a wife who had been in Europe . . .

"Item: When the stock market crashed, big-time Broadway producer Al Woods was in London, opening a show. He phoned his missus in New York to tell her that he had a million bucks in cash hidden under the floorboards of their house, and not to worry about a thing. When he got home, guess what? That's right, Bub—it was gone, and so was she . . ."

As the broadcast continues, we see Owney Madden, listening in his office, an amused look on his face.

We also see a bunch of very dangerous-looking men sitting around a hotel room, listening to the broadcast while they clean and check their pistols and tommy guns. They get a big laugh out of the Al Woods story.

"Mae West sleeps in a black nightgown. So you can't find her, one presumes . . .

"Orchids to Ben Bernie and his lads at the Rainbow Room . . . WW woves their Whippling Whythm. . . .

"And a big Scallion to the bank on Fifth Avenue that has invited their employees to vote for Hoover . . . or else!

"Franklin Roosevelt's maw is okaayy America! She's not afraid to dunk her doughnut in her coffee . . .

"Item: Five planeloads brought a small army of machine gats from Chicago. One midtown hotel has been turned into a virtual arsenal, and all because Mad Dog Coll is giving everyone here a headache. This is Walter Winchell in New York. I'll be back in a flash with a flash."

On hearing this last item, Owney Madden looks up sharply. The bunch of hoods in the hotel room give each other surprised, angry looks.

We hear anonymous radio music. We see a man, VINCENT COLL, walk cautiously into a drugstore, look around, and go to a phone booth in the back. He lifts the receiver, drops in a nickel, as three men rush in and blast the booth with machine-gun fire.

Walter, walking along Broadway. A police car pulls up to the curb and CAPTAIN JOHNNY BRODERICK calls to him.

"Hiya, Johnny . . . boys . . ."

"I thought you might be interested to know that Vincent Coll just got sprinkled in a drugstore over on West Twenty-sixth Street."

Walter's face lights up. "Oh baby! What a scoop!"

Walter, in The Stork Club with Billingsley and Runyon, is congratulating himself.

"Every newspaperman's dream come true. I'm telling you, boys, I scooped the pants off those so-called crime reporters. If I knew who pulled the trigger, I'd give 'em a medal. Crime reporters! Hmpff! Finger snap in face!"

"You don't exactly have to be Sergeant York to machine-gun a guy in a phone booth," Runyon says.

The phone rings.

"Yes, this is Winchell . . ."

He turns absolutely white. He looks scared to death.

"Hey, who is this? Now just wait a minute . . . Hello . . . Hello . . ."

He lets the phone drop.

"Damon, they're gonna kill me!"

"Who was that?" Runyon says.

"They're gonna kill me. Me!"

"You better call the Big Man," Billingsley says.

Owney Madden's office. Walter is slumped down in a chair, chewing his knuckles. Madden is finishing up a call.

"What the hell do you expect?" he's saying. "The guy's a newspaperman. Nobody's hurt except the Mad Dog, and he had it coming. . . . Yeah, well, you *make* them understand. He's a personal friend of mine. And Lucky's." He hangs up.

"All right, Walter, listen. They're sore as hell, naturally. But I think I fixed it."

"Jesus, Owney, thanks."

"See, the question we all wanna know is, who told you?"

"Aw, you know I can't tell you that. I gotta protect my sources."

"Yeah. And I gotta protect mine. The way I figure it, there's only one person close enough and dumb enough, and that's Texas."

Walter looks at the floor.

"Just a yes or no," Madden says. "Nothin'll happen to her. You know that."

Walter looks at Madden, shrugs.

"Right," Madden says. "There's just one thing."

"What?" Walter says.

"I can't give you a hundred percent on this deal. Some hothead wants to blow you down, that's out of my hands. You been working too hard. Maybe you oughta take a little vacation. You ever been to Miami?"

We see a headline: WALTER WINCHELL IS ILL. HIS COLUMN WILL RESUME SOON.

We see a cold, wet corner of Broadway. The street sounds are distant, dissociated. A ghostly newspaper delivery truck passes, a heavy bundle of papers floats down from the back and hits the sidewalk beside a newspaper stand with a dull, echoing thud like a heartbeat. An old man in a cloth cap and a shabby raincoat, bent over, cuts the string that binds the papers. Several papers blow away. He lifts his head, and we see that it's Walter.

A group of laughing people come by: Runyon, Hellinger, Billingsley, June, and Ed Sullivan.

"Hey, Pop, gimme the *Mirror*," Sullivan says.

"Yes sir," Walter says, folding a paper and handing it to him. Sullivan gives him a dollar and waits. June nudges him. "Oh, all right, keep the change," Sullivan says.

"Thank you, sir," Walter says.

Walter sits up in bed with a moan that wakes June. Palm trees, sinister in the moonlight, can be seen through the windows, rustling in the breeze.

"Walter?" June says.

"Oh . . . oh baby," Walter says. He begins to sob uncontrollably. She holds him and cradles his head.

· · ·

Lindy's, late night. The Press Agents are sitting around.

First P.A., glancing over the column: "Who the hell is J. Edgar Hoover? He's got the whole column."

"Read it and find out," Wolfie says.

First P.A.: "Why the hell should I read it? Hoover ain't my client."

Third P.A.: "Y'know, I hate to admit it, but it's pretty boring when Walter's out of town."

"Awww . . .," Wolfie says, "he misses his widdle Walter."

First P.A.: "I called that prick up today. Gus Edwards is trying to make a comeback and I figured, since Gus gave Walter his start in vaudeville, you know . . ."

Third P.A.: "And Walter said, 'Tell Gus to go fuck himself.' "

First P.A.: "You were listening in."

Third P.A.: "That Walter's got a heart of gold."

"Yeah," Wolfie says. "Hard and yellow."

We see a banner on the *Mirror*: WALTER WINCHELL RETURNS ON MONDAY.

Walter, thrilled to be back in harness, walks energetically into the newsroom. Everybody greets him.

"Did you miss me?" he says.

"Every day was like a year," someone says.

But something is going on; reporters give each other sly, significant looks. Walter is oblivious of the slightly conspiratorial atmosphere. He breezes into the office.

A kid sticks his head in the door. "Boss wants to see you, Mr. W."

"Right away," Walter says. He almost dances from his office to the door marked *Managing Editor*, gives the door a perfunctory knock, and barges right in.

Sitting there behind the Managing Editor's desk is Emile Gauvreau. Walter freezes.

"If this is a practical joke, it ain't funny."

"It's no joke," Gauvreau says. There isn't a shred of friendliness to their mutual enmity.

"This is an outrage!" Walter yells. "Why wasn't I told?"

"Mr. Hearst and I wanted to surprise you. You, Mr. Know-It-All."

"Yeah? Well, I've got a big fat surprise for both of you," Walter says, turning to leave.

"He won't take your call," Gauvreau says.

"Oh yes he will."

"Oh no he won't. I told Mr. Hearst that you wouldn't like it if he hired me. And do you know what he said?"

"No," Walter says in a mocking, hateful tone. "What did he say?"

"He said that *he* owned this newspaper, and, in fact, that he owned you, and that what you liked or didn't like was of no interest to him whatsoever. He said to tell you that in future you're not to bring any more of your gangster friends into his newsroom. Mr. Hearst further insists that you be restricted to your office, and that you leave the journalists here alone. Apparently, he's afraid you'll contaminate them. If I need to see you, I'll send for you. As for Mr. Hearst, you are not to attempt to see him for any reason."

"You lying prick."

"He said, I'm quoting him now, 'Winchell seems to satisfy the degraded whims of our readers, but I don't like the man. I don't want to see him again, ever. Keep him far away from me.' "

Gauvreau's office, Walter pacing up and down, furious.

"What do you care? If I say that Trixie Fuckola is vacationing in Florida and she hasn't been south of Brooklyn in ten years, who's hurt? The reader doesn't know, and Trixie's happy because she got her name in the column."

"What price glory?" Gauvreau says.

"Wouldn't you love to know," Walter says.

Walter, frustrated, at his most predatory, is walking down a street, looking for trouble. He spots Irving Hoffman.

"Hey, just a minute . . . I want to talk to you," Walter says, grabbing Irving's arm. "I see you've been leaking stuff to Ed Sullivan."

"Only the stuff you don't want," Irving says. "And anyway, I'm not leaking it. I'm giving it."

"Leaking, giving, what's the difference? You're too frigging friendly with that yutz. I want you to drop him."

"Aw, Walter, you know I can't do that."

"Can't, or won't?"

"Won't," Irving says. "And I'm surprised at you for asking. In fact, you're not even asking."

Irving isn't exactly angry, only incredibly firm. Walter is abashed.

"Aw, come on Irving . . ."

"Really, Walter. You're not happy unless you've got an enemy. You ought to be ashamed of yourself."

"Okay, okay," Walter says. "I'm ashamed."

"Good," Irving says pleasantly. "I'll see you around."

Lindy's Restaurant, late night. A bunch of Press Agents, essentially the same crew we have seen earlier, including Irving and Wolfie.

"I loved that," Wolfie says, "the prick, calling himself Winchell the Magnificent in the column."

"He toned it down," Irving says.

"Yeah, to Winchell the Great," one of them says.

"Go on," Irving says. "Last month you were singing the blues because he was out of town. . . . 'I miss Walter, it's boring without Walter.' "

"What is it with you?" Wolfie says. "He treats you like shit and you love him."

"He doesn't treat me like shit," Irving says. "You, maybe."

"He treats everyone the same," someone says.

"Yeah. Like shit," Wolfie says. "Irving, you must really have something on him. Irving knows where the bodies are buried."

"I don't know where you get your ideas," Irving says.

"Klein's Basement."

"Wolfie's sore 'cause he's out on his ass."

"What, again?" Irving says.

"He sent Walter a gag that he already ran in the column two weeks ago."

"Boy, are you a shmuck."

"I really hate that son of a bitch," Wolfie says. "I'm sorry those dagoes didn't rub him out."

"Hey, have a heart," one of them says. "His kid died, for Christ's sake."

"Yeah," Wolfie says. "And he got three columns out of it. What kind of a man is that? Believe me, I feel as bad about his kid as he does."

"Bite your tongue," Irving says.

Walter, alone in his office, late at night. A single lamp focuses light on his desk. We see the materials for his column spread around, and a photograph of a little girl, GLORIA.

He opens the desk drawer and takes out a child's shoe. He

caresses it, kisses it, lays it down tenderly, and begins typing frantically.

We hear the sound of typing fading out, and see Walter and Irving in Walter's car, late at night.

"You really ought to take a break," Irving says.

"And do what? Sit around and tear my kishkas out? I gotta keep myself busy . . . now more than ever."

"How's June?"

"Aw, she's a toughie, Irving. I thought only Jewish women know how to bury their children. Look, look at this . . . I gotta show you this." He pulls over under the light of a street-lamp and holds up his hand. We see that he is wearing a ring. It looks tacky, cheap.

"A woman in St. Louis sent this to me," Walter says. "She wanted me to wear it as a keepsake for Gloria." His voice suddenly heaves with emotion. "Must have cost, what, two–three bucks, tops . . . You couldn't buy that kind of sentiment in Tiffany's . . . Some people, Irving, I'm telling you, they got hearts the size of the whole damn country."

We hear the sound of typing, see the lead paragraph from the column, hear Walter's excited voice reading:

FLASH! SCOOP!! EXCLUSIVE!!! THE WWS ANTICIPATE A BUNDLE FROM HEAVEN THIS SUMMER!!!!

Walter, in his office, on the phone.

"Cute, Quentin, but I can't use it. *Who* won't let me? You're nuts. No, Mr. Gauvreau is no longer with this organization . . . Yeah, you might say that . . . [He laughs, an echo of triumph.] Even Hearst doesn't touch my column now. Yeah, and he knows it, too. It's just that Germany's a little off my beat . . . You wrote *that* and they won't let you print it? Of course I know who Adolf Hitler is! [He covers the mouthpiece and speaks to his secretary.] Dotty, who the hell is Adolf Hitler? [Uncovers the mouthpiece.] All right, send it over to me, I'll give it a look-see."

Walter and June, in a movie theatre. They are watching the cartoon, which features a bird named Walter Finchell. Walter, in the audience, is knocked out by it, stamping and whistling, as we hear the commentary: "*And so, Broadway's little magpie flies home to his nest with every little trifle he can gather.*"

The cartoon ends, and the newsreel begins. We see Adolf Hitler addressing a Nazi rally. Walter can't believe what he's seeing.

"Is he kidding?" he says loudly to June. "What is he, a *fruit*? Lookit that." Walter rolls his eyes up as Hitler does, wriggles his hips. "Guy's a frigging pansy!"

People start shushing him.

"Aw, nuts," Walter says, rising and turning around. "Shush yourselves. Come on, let's get out of here."

Walter and June walk up the aisle. Hitler's ranting follows them out.

These broadcast items overlap, giving the effect of wave after wave of rising wrathful invective.

Walter broadcasting:

"Good evening, Mr. and Mrs. America and all the ships at sea! This is Walter Winchell in New York. Let's go to press!

"A piece calculated to wake you up screaming: Quentin Reynolds's report in the *Saturday Evening Post* on Adolf Hitler's dream for a new Germany—particularly his plans for Germany's million and a quarter Jews."

·   ·   ·

Walter, broadcasting:

"For those of you who have eyes but see not: It's all right there in black and white in Hitler's book, *Mein Kampf*. That's German for My Struggle . . ."

Walter, broadcasting, hammering:

"A group calling itself Nazi Jews supports Hitler in Germany, and gives the Nazi salute at all their meetings. What's their slogan, 'Down with Us'?"

Walter, broadcasting:

"To Walter Winchell, care of CBS: 'What are you doing next weekend, sweetie? Would you like to spend it with me? I think you're cute. Love, Adolf Hitler.' Maybe they should call him Adele Hitler . . ."

Walter, broadcasting, looking at the front page of a German newspaper with a headline and photo of Winchell:

"Headline, *Volkischer Beobachter*, Hitler's special paper: A new enemy of the new Germany, Walter Winchell. And it says here that my listeners and readers are morons. How do you like *that*, Mr. and Mrs. America?"

We see the name plaque on an office door, reading: *Washington Times-Herald, Eleanor Patterson, Publisher and Prop.*

Standing behind her desk is CISSIE PATTERSON, a tough, well-preserved, spoiled, and alcoholic woman in middle age. She exudes mindless, selfish power. With her is WILLIAM RANDOLPH HEARST and a STENOGRAPHER. Hearst is sitting comfortably in an armchair, his legs stretched out. In all of the following, he seems little more than amused. He has the ice-blue noncommittal eyes of a wolf.

"Can't you control that crazy little kike?" Cissie Patterson says, petulantly, like a frustrated child.

"I could, Cissie, but it wouldn't be in my best interests to do so," Hearst says.

"Ever since Franklin Double-Crossing Jewsevelt got his hooks into him he's been ranting like a Red. . . . These attacks on Germany are embarrassing."

"I would agree with you there," Hearst says. But we see a flicker of distaste at Cissie Patterson's anti-Semitic ranting.

"I wouldn't be surprised to find out that he's in the pay of the British Government."

"No, not Winchell," Hearst says. "He'd never take a dime."

"Well, this newspaper is cutting more and more of his column. Yesterday," she says peevishly, "we left it out completely."

"It's your newspaper, Cissie."

"He's only read by the servants, anyway."

"Then there are a lot of servants in this country," Hearst says. "But I agree with you about this German thing. I don't mind his vulgar little theatrical gossip, but foreign affairs are really our concern."

He speaks to the Stenographer.

"Take this down and circulate it to all offices: 'Please edit Winchell very carefully, and leave out any dangerous and disagreeable paragraphs. . . .' Send that out at once."

"Yes, Mr. Hearst," the Stenographer says, and leaves.

"Happy?" Hearst says dryly.

"I'll be happy when Roosevelt is dead and Winchell's in hell," Cissie Patterson says.

Walter, at his desk, riffling through various newspapers that carry the column in syndication. The column is reduced in all of them. He's holding up the phone, yelling, "I don't give two shits, get me Mr. Hearst immediately!

"Daddy? What the hell is going on? . . . You trying to louse me up? Since when do you take orders from a crazy drunk like Cissie Patterson . . . She's for anything that's against the American people . . . That's what *you* think, Daddy. Get yourself another boy!"

He slams down the phone.

Driving, late at night, with Runyon.

"I just don't believe in biting the hand that feeds me," Runyon is saying. "Hearst always wins. Always has, always will."

"Why, that fat cold-blooded goy bastard. He's a bigger Hitler than Hitler!" He's becoming hysterical. "My fangs have been removed! Jesus, Damon . . . what if I lose my column! I'd just be another shtunk, just another loudmouth in a night-club!" He's on the verge of tears.

"Aw, come on, Walter," Runyon says. "Pull yourself together now."

Night, Central Park West. Walter and Runyon, in Walter's car. They see a big crowd on the sidewalk, a couple of police cars. Walter pulls over.

An automobile has jumped the curb and is piled up against a building. In the center of the crowd, a woman kneels beside a man. He's in shock, and is groaning, over and over: "Oh, my chest hurts . . . my chest hurts bad . . . my chest hurts bad."

We hear the sound of an ambulance siren approaching. The woman looks up and recognizes Walter.

"Shhhh, honey," she says to the man. "Look, it's Walter Winchell."

"Hello, Walter," the man says. "Walter, my chest hurts bad."

Walter's frustration and self-pity vanish in the instantaneous recognition of his power and fame. His face lights up with an almost terrifying smile.

Lindy's, late night. The P.A.s.

First P.A. (Reading from the column, in cruel imitation of Winchell): "The editor of this paper wants to know what it's like to be the daddy of a son . . ."

Wolfie: "Sure, sure . . ."

First P.A.: "Well, it feels just wonderful. . . . He has his father's blue eyes and his mother's sweet disposition. . . ."

"Thank God it isn't vicey-versy!" one of them says.

(Over this we see Walter and Walter Jr., an infant. Walter, like almost any Jewish father, picks the baby up and plants a fervent kiss on the tush.)

First P.A.: "He googles and gurgles, and we understand every word of it. . . . He tastes like honey and smells like gardenias. . . ."

Third P.A.: "Jason, Jason, bring the basin. . . ."

First P.A. (Reading): "Now he says he's the American Hitler would most like to hang."

Wolfie: "Sort of makes Hitler sound like one of the boys . . . (To extremely Jewish waiter) Hey, Max, Walter says the Nazis are coming to get you."

Third P.A.: "They get Max, they'll get you, too."

Wolfie: "What're you gonna do when Hitler waltzes in here some night, Max?"

Max (Shrugs): "I'll chenge mine name."

Walter, broadcasting:

"Good evening, Mr. and Mrs. America and all the ships at

sea. Let's go to press! . . . The German Ambassador in Washington is now flipping only half the Nazi salute at affairs of state, having earned frowns for the full gesture . . . He'll find out eventually that the thing is cut-rate everywhere outside of Germany . . ."

Walter, broadcasting:
"Fritz Kuhn, who poses as a chemist for a motor magnate in Detroit, is Hitler's number-one secret agent in the United States . . . secret until now, that is."

(We see FRITZ KUHN, a wildly arrogant man, listening. He seems amused, flattered, to hear his name.)

"He should get together with a certain female newspaper publisher in Washington—the initials of her paper are the T.H. They could make beautiful music together . . . She's the one who wants to know why I keep looking under the bed for Nazis. Because I keep finding them, lady . . ."

(We see Cissie Patterson, pacing back and forth in front of her radio, holding a drink. When she hears the reference to her, she throws the drink at her radio.)

Against the following segments of Walter broadcasting, we see people across the country listening intently:
We see various American families sitting around radios in their living rooms, some joined by their neighbors.
Men in a tavern, lined up along the bar, quiet during the broadcast.
Guests at a formal dinner, looking toward the radio beyond the head of the table.

A townhall meeting, interrupted while the radio is turned on.

Showgirls in their dressing room.

A Hollywood mogul (Darryl F. Zanuck), stopping a screening to catch the broadcast.

June, with Walda and Walter Jr. We see a drink on the table near her.

Franklin Roosevelt in his office, smiling.

A sailor in a radio room at sea.

A man listening on a car radio as he drives across the country. We see the car, small in an overhead shot, and the headlights illuminating the night. We hear Walter's voice, hammering, insisting, hypnotizing, until we get the feeling that just about everyone in America on this night is listening to Walter Winchell.

"Top U.S. Nazi Fritz Kuhn, who I reported last week was Hitler's number-one man in America, is the head of the thousand-strong—and growing every day—German-American Bund. His job: to spread propaganda, chaos, and sabotage throughout our land. He is *still* employed by our biggest car manufacturer . . . How about it, America. Let's show these swastinkers the gate . . ."

(Kuhn, listening, is not amused anymore. He's cold with fury. "Stinking Jew," he says.)

"Next week my broadcast will come from Hollywood."

A Hollywood nightclub, late night. Walter is stepping out of the front doors when a woman, several yards away, steps into the light and throws off her coat. She's naked. She begins to run toward Walter, as a man in a trenchcoat, holding a press camera, moves in for a picture. Walter sizes up the situation in an instant, covers his face with his hat, and ducks back inside the door. The naked woman runs up to the glass door, as Walter thumbs his nose at her.

Walter, broadcasting:
"By the way, Fritz Kuhn, and all your bungling Bundist buddies, your oh-so-clumsy attempt to entrap and blackmail me was a miserable failure, as you must know by now. Nuts to you, Nazi . . ."

New York, evening. Walter is inside a barbershop, surrounded by P.A.s, cronies.
He leaves, walks up the street, past an alleyway.
"Winchell?" someone says.
"Yeah," Walter says.
Two men step from the alley, grab him, and pull him into the darkness.
"You kikes make too much noise," one of them says. He speaks with a marked German accent.
They beat Walter, who falls groaning to the sidewalk, then they run.

Police Headquarters, Johnny Broderick's office. Walter is dabbing at his face with a wet cloth. He's bruised, his lip is split and swollen, a tooth is broken.
"How do you know they were Nazis?" Broderick says. "Did zey shpeak mit une t'ick Chairman ogzent?"
"I'm telling you, Johnny, it was them!"
"Maybe I'm not big enough mentally, but I can't quite grasp it. All the toes *you* step on . . ."
"They called me a dirty Jew," Walter says.

"Okay, okay, we'll find them. But *you* carry a gun. I'll get you a permit."

"I don't like to fool around with rods," Walter says.

"You really *are* Jewish, aren't you?" Broderick says.

The Stork Club, late night. As Walter enters, he sees a gloomy-looking MAN in the lobby.

"How are you, Jake?" Walter says.

"Great!" Jake says flatly.

"You should notify your face immediately," Walter says.

As he walks on, he's stopped by a weak-looking, handsome, quite drunk YOUNG MAN.

"I must get to Tarrytown at once," he says. "Will you buy this cigarette case from me?"

"Sorry, kid," Walter says, "I can't use a cigarette case." He walks past the young man.

"Who was that?" someone says.

"Café society," Walter says.

The young man stops Billingsley.

"Sherman, will you lend me fifty dollars?"

"I will not," Sherman says.

"Well . . . give me five then."

"Please, William, I'm very busy."

"Then give me a nickel."

Billingsley stops. "Now I'm curious. What're you going to do with a nickel?"

"Call a limousine," the man says. "I can charge it to my mother."

Table 50, The Stork Club. Walter and Runyon.

"Sure, there's going to be a war," Walter says. "It's just a matter of time."

"That's what the morning line says."

"That's what the President thinks, too," Walter says, "but he asked me not to say so."

Billingsley walks by.

"Hey, Sherm," Walter calls. "I hear the Maharajah of Jaipur had a little trouble getting in here last night."

"I just figured he'd be happier at El Morocco," Billingsley says. "Johnny Perona likes that type better than I do."

"What type is that?" Runyon says.

"Polo players," Billingsley says, moving on.

"Sherman wouldn't know a type if it bit him," Runyon says.

Time lapse; it's past midnight. Irving and one or two others have joined the table.

"Johnny Hoover says most crime in America is due to corrupt officials," Walter is saying.

"Gosh," Runyon says. "And who does he say is corrupting them?"

"Runyon and me are going down for the Hauptmann trial tomorrow," Walter says.

"You going to cover it, Damon?" Irving says.

"You know me . . . never miss a good show."

"I'd like to throw the switch on that kraut bastard personally," Walter says.

"After the usual formalities, of course," Runyon says.

"I'll give him formalities . . . I'll give him some frigging formalities," Walter says.

"They're calling Walter the thirteenth member of the jury," Runyon says.

Walter nudges Runyon, nods toward the dance floor.

"My favorite couple," he says. "His wrists are as loose as her morals."

"They're getting married," Irving says.

"Serves them both right," Walter says.

"Some of these so-called debutantes . . . 'Debutramps' is more like it." We see him scribble this word down.

"Remember when girls used to cough if you blew smoke in their face?" Damon says.

Wolfie comes up to the table. He's very drunk. He drops to one knee and grabs Walter's hand so suddenly that Walter doesn't resist.

"What's the bit, Wolfie?"

"Walter," Wolfie says, "I always wanted to tell you . . . to go and fuck yourself."

"Oh ho," Walter says, and starts to laugh and shake his head as if to say, "Oh boy, are you in trouble," as Wolfie elaborately plants a kiss on Walter's ring.

"I'm just kissing your ring so you won't have to stand up."

"God, are you gonna hate yourself in the morning," Walter says, still laughing.

"Let the morning bring what may," Wolfie says drunkenly. "As long as it's *Fuck You Walter Winchell* tonight." He looks at the ring. "You know, a guy with your dough shouldn't wear cheap jewelry."

The change in Walter from amused forbearance to cold insane rage is instantaneous and dramatic. He pulls his hand back, bares his teeth and yells, "Get him out of here! Get him away! Don't you ever let him in here again!"

HAUPTMANN TRIAL. We see a montage sequence of head-lines, the Winchell column, Walter broadcasting; the court-room packed to overflowing, various witnesses testifying, the courtroom grounds like a carnival, Hauptmann himself sitting calm and arrogant, Walter and Runyon in the room watching it all.

. . .

Walter is driving Runyon back to New York after a day at
the trial.

"I know we got a system, but sometimes, between you and
me, it's just a waste of time and money."

"The show must go on," Runyon says.

"Sure, sure, but that kraut is so frigging guilty it isn't funny."

"I wonder."

"What's that, a joke, Damon?"

The car pulls up in front of a roadside diner.

A big blonde WAITRESS is taking their order.

"Gimme some scrambled eggs," Walter says. "And a bagel."

"We ain't got that," the Waitress says.

"No bagels, and this is America," Walter says. "Just some
toast then. And tell the cook to go easy on the eggs. I want
'em scrambled, not black and blue."

She looks vacantly at him.

"I can see I'm really killing her," Walter says to Damon.
"Hey, honey, don't you know who I am?"

"No. Who are you?"

"Well, don't you read the *Mirror?*"

"Naw," she says. "Sometimes I look at the *News*, if it gets
left."

"Well, do you listen to the radio?"

"Don't everybody?"

Walter is almost jumping up and down in his seat. "Did
you ever listen to Winchell?"

"Naw. Most of the time I just like Hawaiian music."

Back in the car, driving into the city.

"Jesus Christ, what a dumb bunny," Walter is saying.
"Mostly I like Hawaiian music. . . . Yaka Hula Hinky
Dula . . ." He's waving his hands. "God damn it, Runyon,

people are dumb. Sometimes I just can't get it through my head that people are so frigging dumb!"

A radio studio. Walter, broadcasting. (In this moment, speaking this one line, he is uncharacteristically still and serious. It's as though he is speaking a deep personal truth for once, without "business" or hyperbole):
"The spotlight sheds a poison, and no one has found the antidote to it yet."
The "business" returns: "And so, from ocean to ocean, with lotions of love, this is Walter Winchell, your New York correspondent, who knows that all the lights on Broadway are never as bright as the candle in the window when you come home."

The front lawn, the Winchell home in Scarsdale. Walter is sitting in a lawn chair. WALDA is playing, the birds are singing, June brings iced tea. Walter stares dead ahead, bored out of his mind.

We hear Walter singing an old song from his vaudeville days:

> America, I love you,
> You're like a sweetheart of mine.
> From ocean to ocean
> For you my devotion
> Is touching each boundary line . . .

As we cut to:

The elevator of the St. Moritz Hotel; noon. Walter and a YOUNG WOMAN. She is very upset; Walter is abashed.
"Listen, honey, I'm sorry already," he says.

"Yeah, you're sorry," she says. "You promised."

"Oh, will you stop that, 'You promised, you promised,' " Walter says. "It happens."

"Not to me."

"Oh, sure."

"I mean it," she says.

"Well, listen," Walter says. "Welcome to the club. You're in illustrious company. You'd be surprised."

"You better do something for *me* now."

Walter pats her on the arm, suddenly quite tender. "Don't worry, sugar. You just watch the column."

The elevator doors open, and they step into the lobby. They meet a tall, expensively dressed man, FRANK COSTELLO. (We don't really have to know anything about him specifically; we see that he is powerful, suave, and very sinister. His smooth good manners with the young woman are in keeping with the style of a man who derives a large part of his income from prostitution.)

"Hello, Walter," Costello says.

"Hey, Francisco," Walter says. "Honey, this is Mr. Costello."

"It's a very great pleasure to meet you," Costello says to the woman. "You're a very sweet young lady. Walter, what do you hear from your friend John Hoover?"

"Oh, he's keeping himself busy," Walter says.

"That's good," Costello chuckles. "There's a horse called Siam running at Pimlico this afternoon. I forget which race, but he's the winner. Seven-to-one, maybe better. I know Hoover likes the bangtails. Pass it along."

"Should I tell him where I got it?" Walter says, provocatively.

"Please yourself," Costello says.

. . .

Walter, broadcasting:

"The *New York Times* describes Toots Shor as an 'ovoid man' . . . That means you're egg-shaped, Toots.

"When Joan Crawford fox-trots with Bruce Cabot, she shuts her eyes and shudders all over . . .

"J. Edgar Hoover, America's Top Cop, has been looking at a family-size house in Georgetown . . . A bride? . . .

"Ed Sullivan believes two heads are better than one . . . Not when they're on the same neck, Ed . . .

"Mrs. F.D.R. is taking rhumba lessons . . ."

We see Walter in close-up, a heightening of intensity.

". . . Louis Buchalter is the man that everybody wants to talk to, but is he popular? Not exactly. In the days when he ran the notorious Murder Incorporated, his friends—and what friends—called him Lepke, but they haven't seen him around lately. Shy? Certainly—gun shy. Listen, Louie, you know and I know that it's only a matter of time. If your old pals find you, you're dead. If Special Prosecutor Dewey finds you, you'll wish you were dead. If you're listening, Louie, contact me. I can offer you a better deal.

"With lotions of love, and hugs and kisses for Mr. and Mrs.—America, that is—this is your New York correspondent Walter Winchell, who wants to remind Mussolini—just because your country is shaped like a boot doesn't mean you have to act like a heel!"

Walter, broadcasting:

"Lepke, if you're listening, and I'll bet you are, it's not too late. Surrender to me, and I can guarantee you safe conduct. If you have a better offer than that, by all means take it. I have the word of the District Attorney and the Director of the FBI that every consideration will be shown to you, if you surrender. Think it over, Louis . . . while you still have time."

Walter, broadcasting:
"Lepke, I have a message for you from J. Edgar Hoover. It's short and it's sweet. If you're coming in, come in now. This is it. It's your last chance . . ."

The Hollywood Barbershop, late afternoon. Walter is being shaved. In the next chair, another customer is being lathered. A dark, tough-looking MAN comes in.
"Winchell?" he says.
Walter appraises him. "Yes, I am he," he says.
"I wanna talk to you."
"So talk."
"In private."
Walter looks up at his barber, jerks his head toward the customer in the next chair.
"Yes, Mr. Winchell," the barber says. Then, to the other customer, "You heard Mr. Winchell."
"Yes, I heard him," the customer says, "and I don't give a good god damn. Let him go to his office if he . . ."
"Out!" Walter yells.
The two barbers lift the man from his chair and move him out onto the street, still lathered.
"Is this private enough?" Walter says. "Or should I leave too?"
"Lepke wants to come in," the man says.

Walter, on the phone to Hoover.
"Johnny, listen, Lepke's ready. He'll give himself up to you if I bring him in."

"Make your deal," Hoover says. "I'll come up."

"Sit tight," Walter says. "I'll let you know."

Night, the Bronx. Walter, driving, pulls up in front of a synagogue. A MAN comes out, slides into the seat next to Walter.

"This ain't your car, Mr. Winchell," he says.

"Too many people know my car. Johnny Hoover thought I ought to drive this instead."

The man thinks this over, nods. "Switching cars. That's cute. You and Hoover ever do any bank jobs?"

"It's for Lepke's safety. And mine. Where are we going?"

"Down Tenth Avenue. I get out at Thirty-fourth Street. You go around to Ninth and Twenty-ninth. Pull up in front of the drugstore and wait. And listen . . . when you see Lepke, give him this for me."

He reaches into his pocket and takes out a mezuzah on a gold chain and gives it to Walter.

Walter, alone in the car, the motor running, in front of a drugstore. LEPKE steps out of an alley, gets into the car.

"Hello, Lepke," Walter says. He is very nervous, as is Lepke.

"Hello," Lepke says. "Remember me?"

"Remember you?"

"Yeah. I was at P.S. 181 the same time you were. A few years behind."

"You're kidding," Walter says.

"No. I was scared of you."

"Scared of *me*?" Walter laughs.

"Yeah. You had some pretty tough friends."

Walter is laughing, from nerves and surprise. "I still do," he says.

·   ·   ·

Night. Walter's car pulls into a warehouse district. There are several cars; a van; G-men with guns; HOOVER. Walter stops the car, and the G-men surround it.

"Johnny Hoover, this is Louis Lepke," Walter says.

"Pleased to meet you," Lepke says, holding out his hand to Hoover. Hoover is actually more nervous than anybody else there. He nods, and clumsily puts the cuffs on Lepke's wrists.

"Well, I guess that's it," Walter says.

The G-men push Lepke toward the van, a little rougher than is necessary under the circumstances.

"Hey, wait a minute," Walter says. He takes the mezuzah out of his pocket and hands it to Lepke. "Your friend asked me to give this to you."

"Thanks," Lepke says. He kisses the mezuzah emotionally.

Walter's car screeches to a stop in front of a phone booth. He dials quickly. "Hello! Herb, it's me. Yeah. You better wipe the front page! I got a big one!"

We see the editor, HERB.

"It better be awfully big, Walter. The Germans have just invaded Poland."

We see Walter's face; shock, then indignation, then resignation.

Walter, antsy, pacing furiously back and forth in front of the phone booth. He stops, brightens.

Walter, back in the booth, telephoning.

"Hiya, honey," he says.

We can hear June's voice indistinctly. She is hysterical.

"We did it. I just brought Lepke in," Walter is saying. "And you won't believe this, the goddamnedest thing, the biggest scoop of my career and . . ."

June's voice, like her hysteria, is rising.

"He what? Is he all right? . . . Did the doctor come?"
June is yelling at him. We hear, "You're never home!"
"All right, all right, I'll be right there. Yes, yes, darling.
Give him a big kiss for me." He hangs up.

As he leaves the phone booth, a COP walks by.

"Hiya, Mr. Winchell," he says.

"Hi," Walter says. He's sheepish, defeated, vulnerable. "My
kid just fell out of a tree and cut his knee open. The wife's
mad as hell at me."

"Yeah, well, whaddya gonna do, you know?" the Cop says.

AUTUMN 1939

Walter, in his dressing room at NBC. He's pacing around,
glancing at the scraps of paper as they're handed to him. Most
go into his wastepaper basket. He keeps looking out the window, across the alley, into the dressing room of the Radio City
Music Hall Rockettes.

Irving Hoffman sticks his head in.

"You got everything?" he says.

"Everything and more, Oiving," Walter says. "Stick around
for the broadcast."

They go into the broadcast booth, where Walter arranges
the pages over the table. He's incredibly charged up, almost
jumping up and down in his chair.

"You okay?" Irving says.

"I gotta pee."

"So go pee. You got seven minutes."

"Naw. It's better if I do it this way. Gives it more oomph.
It's good show business."

He opens his trousers, sits, stares at the green light.

Irving leaves the studio.

The light turns red, and Walter starts hitting the telegraph key.

"Good evening, Mr. and Mrs. America and all the ships at sea . . . Let's go to press. Flash! The Government of Great Britain did not declare war on the German people. Possibly as a result of this reporter's advice, cabled three days ago to Prime Minister Chamberlain, they have declared war on Adolf Hitler and the Nazis only . . ."

On the other side of the glass a funny look comes over Irving Hoffman's face, a kind of awe that, after all these years, Walter's nerve can still surprise him.

"Since your newsboy advocated the rapid development of a two-ocean Navy, several weeks ago, more than a million and a half letters have poured into Congress supporting the idea. The response has been so strong, it almost woke up several members of Congress . . . Almost . . ."

We see Irving Hoffman again. Something like mild alarm crosses his face.

"Now they are calling me Walter Warmonger, and demanding to know why I don't stick to Broadway, and gossip, and trivial matters. Senator Rip Van Wheeler says that I chant the hymn of hatred every week, and then close with lotions of love . . . Well, Senator, and Colonel Lindbergh, and Congressmen Fish, Rankin, et cetera, all of you Hitler-rooters high and low . . . Black Shirts and Brown Shirts and Silver Shirts . . . to Fritz Kuhn and Gerald L. K. Smith and Father Coughlin . . . my hatred is for America's enemies, abroad and at home, and my love, which is just as fierce, is for those who love freedom. Zzzzanything wrong with that?"

. . .

Irving is now quite uncomfortable.

"I'll stick to Broadway when our elected officials stick to preserving our liberties and protecting our country."

We see a general reaction to the broadcast now, people by their radios.

"I have never had so many battles at once in my entire career. Because I support our President, they call me Franklin Roosevelt's stooge. Because I cherish the Constitution, they call me a fanatic. Because I can see beyond the end of my nose, I am called an alarmist, a demagogue and, yes, a warmonger. My enemies, who I have the honor to share with the President, are hitting us both from every side—mostly from behind. But I don't mind. In fact, I love it. I love a brawl . . . So don't worry, folks. I'm not dizzy. I'm just busy . . .

"However, just for those of you who think I ought to stick to Broadway gossip, here's a little tidbit. . . Honeychile Wilder was out with Rags Ragland Friday night, and on Saturday she was at The Stork Club with Bob Richie. Honeychile's gone from Rags to Richie . . . Oh that Winchell . . .

"With a harsh hymn for the haters, and lotions of love for all *good* Americans, this is Walter Winchell in New York, reminding you that the ride begun by Paul Revere all those years ago has never really ended."

The broadcast light goes off. Walter leaves the booth, holding his trousers up, and is surrounded by fawning press agents and radio people.

"Outta my way," Walter yells, as he runs out of the studio for the bathroom.

Irving sits quietly, reflectively, watching.

The lobby of the St. Moritz Hotel, late morning. Walter and an attractive young woman get off the elevator together and go separate ways. A bunch of Press Agents surround Walter like pilot fish. As they pass through the lobby, the DESK CLERK calls out.

"Mr. Winchell . . . this just arrived for you."

He hands Walter an envelope. Walter opens it, looks it over, and breaks into an exultant laugh.

"Oh ho *ho!*" he says. "Yuk yuk *yuk!*"

"What is it?"

"What is it? As if it's any of your frigging business, this is the latest Hooper Rating Report. And it says that I'm on top! Number one across the land, from ocean to ocean . . . Better than Benny or Crosby or Hope! Bigger than Fibber McGee and Molly! Number One!"

He throws back his head and crows: "*Cock-a-doodle-doo!*"

Waving the rating above his head, he goes out onto the street, still crowing.

"Hi there, Mr. and Mrs. America!" he yells, as people on the street stop. "Did you hear what I said about you last night on the radio? . . . *Cock-a-doodle-doooooo!*"

Dawn, Scarsdale. We hear the fading echo of Walter's "Cock-a-doodle-doo," as we see Walter sound asleep in bed. The bedroom door opens, and June comes in.

"Honey, wake up," she says.

"What time is it?" he says sleepily. We can hear the telephone ringing far away.

"Walter, get up," June says. "There are a million phone calls. The Japanese have attacked Pearl Harbor."

"So what took 'em so long?" he says.

He sits up, puts his arm around her.

"Looks like this is the end of the slow music, kid," he says.

Walter, broadcasting with great force:

"Listen, Adolf and Benito and Tojo—don't think the oceans can protect you . . . We're coming at you now with everything we've got, and it's plenty! We did it before, and we can do it again . . . Okay, America! And okay, F.D.R.!"

Night, The Stork Club. Walter makes a particularly impressive entrance, dressed in the uniform of a Lieutenant Commander in the U.S. Navy. He removes his hat, brushes it tenderly with his sleeve, and hands it to the hat-check girl.

He passes Billingsley and a MAN.

"What the hell is *this*?" the man says.

"That's Walter's contribution to the war of nerves," Billingsley says.

Walter in uniform, dancing with a beautiful WOMAN, the Cub Room.

Walter at Table 50; with him is the Woman, Damon Runyon, etc. Walter is on the phone.

"He did? Oh he do, do he?" He covers the mouthpiece, speaks to Runyon. "Westbrook Pigler says I'm a disgrace to the uniform."

"Oh, I think you look handsome," the woman says.

"Kiss me, Hardy," Runyon says.

Walter hangs up. "First, he calls me a louse in the blouse of journalism. Now he's got his nose up there pretty good with Cissie Lushhead Patterson and those Ku Klux Klan Kongressmen . . . I tell you, sometimes I think America loves me for the enemies I make."

Walter, broadcasting:

"Repeated charges that my commission in the United States Navy was proving to be an embarrassment to our great President prompted me to do the only thing a patriot could do. I personally handed the President my resignation from the Navy. If any of you would like to read it, you can find it easily . . . At the bottom of the President's wastebasket."

Walter, in uniform, at a bond rally. He's auctioning off tickets to a Broadway show. He moves into the crowd waving the tickets over his head. Surrounded by the People, fitting so easily into the place and hour, he seems totally happy.

Over this, we hear him singing to himself, "Any bonds today . . . Here comes the Freedom Man, with his shmuck in his hand, sayin', 'Do you want any bonds today?' "

Lindy's, 1 a.m. Various Press Agents.
First P.A., greeting: "Hey, Greenie, where you been?"
"Las Vegas," Greenie says.
"Where's that, Mexico?" the First P.A. says.
"Naw," someone says. "It's in California."
"It's in Nevada," Greenie says.
"I never heard of it," the First P.A. says.
"You never heard of Las Vegas?" Greenie says.
"No. I never heard of Nevada."
"Walter coming in?" Greenie asks.
"The Admiral is in Rio de Janeiro," the Second P.A. says. "That's in Brazil," he says to the First P.A. "He flew there. In a air-o-plane."

"Walter *flew*?" Greenie says. "I thought he was chicken."
"Now that he's the People's Oracle, he's an eagle."
"The People's Testicle's more like it," the First P.A. says.
"The sore one."

A shot of Sugarloaf Mountain.
A formal banquet dais, Walter in uniform, surrounded by diplomats and Brazilian military. He rises grandly.
"I hear you got an awful lot of coffee in Brazil," he says. "So I'll use it to propose a toast. To the great nations of Brazil and the United States: Never above you. Never below you. Always beside you." He raises his coffee cup and drinks, to big applause.

The kitchen of The Stork Club. A tremendous argument is going on, men screaming at each other in a mix of French, German, Italian, and broken English. It can be heard in the Cub Room. Billingsley storms in, grabs the first two men he sees, and shakes them hard.
"You wanna play war, go enlist. I don't give a shit in which army, either. But if there's any more of this in my club, I'll shoot you myself."

Walter, broadcasting:
"Americans of every race and creed are fighting and dying side by side. A Jap or a Nazi bullet doesn't ask what religion you believe in, or the color of your skin. Yet the worst kind of racial hatred can be heard every day in the halls of Congress . . . Congressman Rankin of Mississippi has particularly honored me this week by attempting to defame me, in language that I would not repeat on the air . . . It's in the Congressional Record, folks . . . Rankin, Hoffman, Wheeler, Reynolds,

Bilbo, Fish, Dies . . . this microphone is always open to you for your defense . . . But then, you don't believe in defense . . . that's in the record, too . . . only in cowardly attack."

Table 50, with Runyon and Billingsley.

"Come on, Walter," Runyon is saying, "I'm a newspaperman, too. What did Rankin actually call you?"

Walter, a big smile, says, "Congressman Rankin called me a little slime-mongering kike."

"You mean in so many words?"

"I mean in those very words. On the floor of the Congress of the United States."

"I don't believe it," Billingsley says.

"Look, even Sherman's shocked," Walter says. "By Sherm, a kike is a Jewish fella who's just left the room."

"Aw, come on, Walter," Billingsley says, blushing.

"It isn't that he *said* it," Walter says. "It's that not one man stood up to object. How do you like that?"

"The Good Lord must love assholes," Runyon says. "He made so many of them."

WALTER JR., ten years old, dressed in a uniform almost identical to his father's, is led into the Cub Room by a Press Agent.

"Sonny boy!" Walter says. "How was the circus? Orchids or Scallions?"

"It was good," the boy says flatly.

"Great! So you had a good time . . ." He switches the question to the P.A.: "He have a good time?"

"Terrific," the P.A. says.

Billingsley comes up to the table. "He wants a drink in here, I'm gonna have to see some I.D."

"The car outside?" Walter asks.

"Ready and waiting," the P.A. says.

"Can't I have dinner with you?" Walter Jr. says, trying to muffle his disappointment.

"Aw, your old pappy's got to work," Walter says.

"I want a Winchellburger," the boy says. Everyone laughs.

"A Winchellburger," Walter says. "When you get home, tell Mrs. Winchell to fix you a Winchellburger. I'll be out Saturday morning. Okay?"

"Yeah," the boy says, clearly hurt.

"Give this to your mommy for me," Billingsley says, handing Walter Jr. a bottle of Sortilège perfume. Walter Jr. and the Press Agent leave.

"That's a good-looking boy, Walter," someone says. "What is he now, fourteen?"

"No," Walter says. "He's ten."

"He looks much older."

"He worries a lot," Walter says.

The street in front of The Stork Club.

The Press Agent waves to a car parked in the street. A couple is stepping out of a limousine. As the limousine pulls away, Walter Jr. throws the bottle of perfume at it with all his strength. Reflexively, the Press Agent grabs him.

"Jesus Christ, kid," he says.

Walter, broadcasting:

". . . and when they cannot slander me in any other way, they say that I'm prejudiced . . . Prejudiced? You bet I'm prejudiced. I'm prejudiced against all those in high office who guessed so wrong before Pearl Harbor. They are still guessing wrong. They worry me. But what worries me most are all the *damned fools* who reelected them."

.   .   .

Irving, sitting outside the booth, sits up with a jerk.

In the control room, the DIRECTOR says, "Oh my God!"

A NETWORK EXECUTIVE, listening at home, drops his head in his hands.

The NBC switchboard goes berserk.

The Network Executive's office. THE SPONSOR, an AGENCY REP, NETWORK PEOPLE, and Walter.

"Walter, you cannot say 'damned' on the radio on Sunday night," the Executive says, barely able to control himself.

"I'm sorry. I thought you could," Walter says.

"And you can't call the voters 'fools,' " the Sponsor says.

"Even if they are?" Walter says.

"Especially if they are," the Executive says.

"I'm only saying what F.D.R. says."

"F.D.R. doesn't have a sponsor," the Executive says.

"What's the matter," Walter says, "haven't you got any faith in your product? I certainly have in mine. So a few people get their noses out of joint, so what? Their enemies will run out and buy your hand lotion. And by the way, F.D.R. does have a sponsor—Mr. and Mrs. America."

"The very people you offended," the Sponsor says.

"Listen, I'm not gonna barber with you," Walter says, rising. "You can't have my teeth."

"Oh Walter . . ."

"I'm not giving you momsers my teeth. My ratings aren't good enough for you, go hire somebody without teeth."

He storms out of the office.

Walter, walking out of the Network Executive's office. He's laughing and shaking his head at how successful his performance was. As the elevator doors open, he breaks into a soft-shoe, singing "Jimmy Valentine," and glides into the elevator.

. . .

The Stork Club, night. The orchestra is playing "Stardust." Walter is on the dance floor with WALDA, seventeen years old and thrilled to be dancing with her father.

Damon watches them from Table 50. A MAN comes by, says hello.

"Walter likes 'em younger and younger," the man says, looking at the dance floor.

"That's his daughter," Runyon says hoarsely. "Walter doesn't like 'em too young. He says they smell of milk."

Over "Stardust" played at fox-trot tempo, we see a montage of newsreels and newspaper headlines, announcing the major events of the closing year of the war. (Over this, we will hear Walter broadcasting, like fragments blowing in and out of static.)

We see newsreel footage of Franklin Roosevelt returning from Yalta, as Walter broadcasts:

"F.D.R.'s physicians say that his health is the best it's been in years. So is America's!"

The footage is slowed down almost imperceptibly. We see F.D.R., obviously a dying man.

Walter in his darkened office, late at night. He's slumped over, with his head in his arms, crying his heart out.

Over this we hear him broadcast:

"The President of the United States is dead. All that was mortal of F.D.R. will now pass from the sight of men. But the things for which he lived, fought, and died will live forever, while there are free men left to draw a breath.

"And now this great burden has fallen to a new President. Harry S. Truman's warm humility has long been his most striking characteristic. His favorite motto: 'It's what you learn after you know it all that counts.' This is the great American that Franklin Delano Roosevelt chose to act as his lieutenant through the final terrible days of war. May God in His tenderness bless and sustain him, till victory is won. This is Walter Winchell in New York."

Table 50. Walter, Runyon, Irving, etc.
Walter's fist crashes down on the table.
"*That's* a President? That's a frigging President?" he yells. "That cunt-faced, crony-assed hicktown crook? And crude? I say, 'How do you do, Mr. President, I'm Walter Winchell,' and he says, 'I know. So what?' I couldn't believe it. I was speechless."

Damon laughs at the very idea.

"Then he says, 'You People did a lot of favors for Franklin Roosevelt . . . I hope you don't expect to collect on them from me.' I kept waiting for him to say it was all a big joke. I told him, I said, 'Listen, I remember when a *President* sat in that chair! Anything I ever did for F.D.R. I did for love, gratis, no charge, ever. A favor for F.D.R. was a favor for America. And whaddya mean by *You People*? . . . You know what he calls Dorothy Schiff? He calls her that damned New York Jew publisher. I tell you, this guy's gonna get it from me . . . *You People* . . . the President of the United States."

"Yeah," Damon says. "Franklin Roosevelt was really crazy about Jews."

"Don't *you* start," Walter yells. "There's too many damn people around already who've got nothing better to do than knife a dead president in the back."

"Hey, I'm sorry . . ."

"They're even trying to knife his widow!"

"Walter, I didn't mean it. Relax."

"Okay," Walter says. "Okay."

. . .

Walter, broadcasting.

Over this, we see shots of New York in the hour before dawn, ending with shots of Walter's car on its nightly rounds.

"America is at peace. Robins are nesting in the air-raid siren atop Radio City. About the only insignia you see is on the shoulders of Park Avenue doormen. But before you relax, remember! The soft peace that follows the hard war has left Europe once again exposed, and we stand with Europe. We have enemies today that were undreamed of ten years ago, and no Commander with the strength or the wisdom to lead us. And where are these new enemies to be found? Why, right here at home, enjoying the full privileges and protections of our great country . . .

"Doctors have ordered Damon Runyon to relax, but nobody bothered to explain the meaning of the word to him . . .

"A listener asks if I know what the S in Harry S. Truman stands for. Brother, I'm still trying to figure out what Harry Truman stands for . . ."

Over these last two items, we see Walter's car, late at night, prowling the streets of New York.

(NOTE: *This sequence of related scenes occurs over a period of four months, from August through November, in the increasingly isolated and intimate capsule of Walter's car. The difficulty that both Walter and Runyon have in saying what they feel is the cause of some awkwardness between them; the alternatives which they find to express those feelings is the source of some tenderness. They certainly could never speak like this if a third party were present.*)

. . .

Walter's car; interior. Runyon is with him in the front seat. He seems exhausted. He often speaks in little more than a hoarse whisper.

"You really ought to stop knocking yourself out," Walter says.

"I don't have much choice," Runyon says. "The divorce cleaned me out."

"That's funny . . . You used to say that paying alimony was like buying oats for a dead horse."

"Only the horse isn't dead," Runyon says.

For a moment Walter doesn't know what to say.

"The black market money's all drying up," he finally says. "Sherman says the take is way down. Different crowd, too."

"I've seen happier kissers at a soda fountain," Runyon says. "Pull over a second, will you?"

"What?" Walter says, drawing up to the curb.

"Cut the motor," Runyon says. "Listen."

Walter cocks his head like a bird, listening. We hear with him the low, steady roar of New York.

"Even at this hour," Runyon says. "Listen to that, will you?"

There is an enthusiasm in this, an awe, that Walter has never heard from Runyon before. He looks at him surprised, not sure if this is a gag or not.

"I'll tell you," Runyon says. "There'll never be another city like this one. Never."

Over shots of the car driving late at night in the September rain, we hear Walter broadcasting:

"To the judges at Nuremberg: When you think of a Jap or a German at war, just think of a murdered child. Now that the Nip and the Nazi are begging for mercy, remember that they showed none to this child. Your reporter sees no problem in how to give them justice. Take them to the nearest wall, and bang bang bang! . . ."

(We see the Winchell column; we see that the page is shared by the Runyon column.)

"Tony DeMarco predicts that the next big dance fad will be the mambo—a zingier form of rhumba which he intro'd last week at the Havana-Madrid . . .

"Comic Bill Conti offers this definition of Sweater Girl— She pulls your eyes over her wool . . .

"Have the *Île de France* and other French luxury liners been taken off their runs to rush troops to Indo-China?

"Damon Runyon's checked out of New York Hospital, awwww better. The doctors said he's been working too hard . . ."

Night; Walter's car. Runyon, his head resting against the window. "If we crashed right now, and both of us were killed, how do you think the headline would read?" he says. "Winchell and Runyon Killed or Runyon and Winchell?"

"Billing doesn't matter much when you're dead," Walter says. He clearly hates the subject of this conversation.

"On the contrary," Runyon says. "That's when it matters most."

"Our stuff's gonna be around a long time after we're gone," Walter says.

"Don't kid yourself. Twenty years, tops, they'll forget we were ever here."

They come to a street corner. Under the streetlight, they see a legless man. His wheelchair has been overturned. He has his hands around the throat of a young man. A few people stand around, hanging back, hypnotized.

"Jesus Christ," Walter says, grabbing for the microphone on his police radio. Runyon stops him.

"Wait a minute," he says. "I've never seen a man strangled before."

"Christ sake, Damon . . ."

The legless man is perfectly calm, smiling, a lighted cigarette dangling from his lips. His hands are incredibly powerful. "Watch," he says, almost to himself. "Watch him go to sleep." The other man is limp on the sidewalk.

Walter and Damon are transfixed. Then a police siren is heard approaching. The witnesses scatter. The legless man releases his victim, rights his wheelchair, hops into it and wheels away. The man on the sidewalk moves, groaning.

"Some busybody called the cops," Damon says. "Well . . . maybe some other time."

Walter's car, driving through an early snowstorm; we hear these broadcast items:

"Hard to b'leev—an Air Force Captain, with more than thirty missions over Tokyo, is working now at the Club 400 —as a busboy! . . ."

(We see the Winchell column. On the same page, in place of the Runyon column: "*Damon Runyon is on vacation.*")

"Ed Sullivan, wrong as usual but moreso, hears that the Sherman Billingsleys have phffffft! Now what rat told that rat that . . . ?

"Damon Runyon's back in the hospital for a quick checkup. Runyon's being ill is like New York Harbor with the Statue of Liberty darkened. . . .

"This is Walter Winchell in New York, who knows it pays to be nice to people on the way up. Success doesn't last forever, but friendship does."

The car, interior; Walter and Damon.

"You know this guy Roney Chester?" Walter says. "He says he's real close to you."

"That's what *he* thinks. Nobody's close to me."

Walter laughs. It's quiet for a moment.

"You know what I think was the worst thing I ever did?" Damon says.

Walter doesn't answer.

"There was a fight manager named Byron Dawes. He was really down on his luck. Mostly because he wasn't a crook. He looked after his boys. He asked me to write about one of his fighters. I knew he was flat broke, but I made him meet me at 21 for lunch to talk about it. I made him pay for the lunch. And I never mentioned his boy in the column. . . . And he was a real good boy, too."

Walter has a deep response to this story, and to the way Runyon has told it, as though he knows what Runyon really wants to say to him.

"What's the worst thing *you* ever did?" Runyon says.

"Jesus, I wouldn't know where to start," Walter says.

"Well, pardner, even if you did, I wouldn't have time to hear it all."

"Listen, Damon, there's nothing wrong with you that a good long rest wouldn't fix."

"And I intend getting it."

"Come on, kiddo . . . Where's the old Runyon?"

"The old Runyon doesn't live here anymore," Damon says.

The Stork Club, early evening. We see Table 50 being set. Paper, pencils, and an orchid are laid at Walter's place; next to that, at Runyon's place, we see pencils and a pad. The notepaper bears the printed heading DAMON RUNYON SAYS.

We see several very brief overlapping scenes at Table 50, to establish that all of Runyon's conversation is now being conducted in writing.

Walter is talking, as usual. Runyon rolls his eyes up and laughs. He writes something down with great firmness, all in caps, with exclamation points, the words underlined several times, and hands the note to Walter.

"Runyon says I'm full of shit," Walter says. "Gee, Damon . . . you don't have to shout."

"The perfect couple," Irving says. "Damon can't talk, and Walter can't shut up."

Everybody laughs; they're both moved by Runyon's courage and relieved that he is being such a good sport.

We see a train speeding through the night, hear music on the sound track suggestive almost of flight and pursuit.

Walter's compartment, the train to Florida.

June is resting, her eyes closed. Walter is staring tensely, morosely, out the window. June opens her eyes and looks at him.

"Hiya, baby," she says.

"Frigging doctors," Walter says. "Goddamn tinpot gods . . . They don't know what the hell they're talking about . . . Some big frigging deal, they are."

June says nothing, but looks at him with real concern and pity.

Runyon's suite, the Hotel Buckingham. It's four o'clock in the morning. A cold rain beats against the windows. In the sitting room, a NURSE is sleeping on the sofa. We hear the sound of typing from the bedroom.

· · ·

Runyon's bedroom. He's sitting at his typewriter. Next to it is the framed photograph of Patrice, his ex-wife. He finishes typing, rolls the paper up, and looks at it. We see that it is a short poem. Over the following movements, we hear Runyon's voice, barely more than a rough whisper, reading this:

> *And so we kneel when darkness comes and pray.*
> *(There's very little we can say)*
> *Lord oh Lord, give us this day.*
> *Be with us.*
> *Stay with us.*

With great effort, he gets up from the table, crosses the room to the wardrobe and slides the wide door open along its track. He goes to a chair facing the wardrobe and drops into it. His face is drawn with the exhaustion of a long, lost battle.

We see the wardrobe: a hundred suits, a hundred pairs of shoes.

Runyon sits, looking at his clothes.

Walter, broadcasting:

"Mr. and Mrs. United States! A very dear friend of mine —a great newspaperman, a great writer, and a very great guy—Damon Runyon, was killed this week by America's Number Two killer—Cancer. It's time we tried to do something to fight this terrible disease. We must fight back, and together we can do it. Won't you send me a penny, a nickel, a dime, or a dollar? All of your money will go directly to the cancer fighters, in Damon Runyon's name. There will be no expenses of any kind deducted."

Walter in Lindy's, with his Press Agent cronies.

". . . Bugsy Siegel sent us eight grand," Walter is saying. "Twenty-five grand from Frank Costello . . ."

Walter, broadcasting:
". . . Twenty bucks from a cab driver in the Bronx . . . and nine thousand pennies from some Brooklyn schoolchildren. Bing, Bob, Frankie, and Dinah have all scheduled benefits for the Damon Runyon Memorial Fund . . ."

Lindy's again, with the Press Agents.
". . . there's this hooker in L.A. who has an exclusive arrangement with Harry Cohn, he thinks. She's moonlighting and sending the money to the Runyon Fund . . ."

Walter, broadcasting:
"When we began, we hoped that fifty thousand dollars or so might be donated. But Mr. and Mrs. America, whose heart is as big and great as our great country, have already made it more than fifteen million."

June, alone at Table 50. She is waiting with obvious impatience for Walter. People at nearby tables are staring openly at her.
A waiter comes by. "Mr. Winchell says he'll be here in ten, maybe fifteen minutes. Can I bring you another drink?"
"That's a good idea," June says. She smiles an exaggerated, somewhat hostile smile at the people who are gaping at her.
Some of them look away.
She picks up the orchid that is lying on the table, delicately removes a petal, pops it into her mouth, and chews it carefully. The others look away, too.

.   .   .

Table 50, June. Half an hour later.

June is drinking, tight.

A MAN and a WOMAN pass the table.

"Hello, Junie," the man says.

June fixes him with a hard look. "Are you speaking to me?" she says. "Because if you are, you've certainly got one hell of a nerve. You rat."

"Aw June," the man says.

"And you're not a very smart rat, either."

"Now you just wait a minute," the woman says.

"I know what you've been saying about Walter," June says. "And you don't even have the guts to put it in your column. I beg your pardon, your so-called column."

"He's only saying what's true," the woman says.

"How do *you* know what's true?" June says.

"Listen, honey, if you don't care that your husband is in bed with every tramp in town . . ."

"They can't all be tramps," June says. "I'm sure some of them are very nice girls."

Walter comes up to the table. He hears this last line.

"And anyway," June says to the man, "since when are *you* such a Boy Scout?"

Walter slides in next to June, laughs at the man.

"Don't look at me, shmendrick. Nobody edits June. Not even me."

The man and his wife move away.

"That frigging jackass," Walter says. "Newspaperman! Hmpf!" He yells after the man, "The only scoop *you* ever got was in an ice-cream soda!"

He hugs June.

"I love you, baby," he says proudly. "Rahlly I do."

Autumn in New York
1947

We hear this played almost like an anthem, a tone too lush, over shots of the city at its most beautiful. The glamour and glory of Walter Winchell's epoch have reached full ripeness, and can only become overripe.

Theatre marquees, nightclub fronts, etc., interspersed with the Winchell column, focusing on column titles and famous names. We hear Walter broadcasting throughout this sequence. Where his style was once pure energy, it sounds merely frantic now, pitched to an audience that has become habituated to him.

"Reason the Russians are so cocky lately is that they allegedly have a Cosmic Ray Bomb. Planning to invite Americans and other nations to demonstrations of the new weapon . . . Insiders unimpressed, claiming we have a weapon that makes the Atom bomb obsolete . . ."

(We see shots of television aerials on Manhattan rooftops, multiplying until they dominate the skyline.)

"Betsy Hart and Tommy Trevain are straining at the leash . . ."

(Crowds standing in front of store windows, watching television.)

"The bouncer at the Mermaid Room is a midget! He quiets unruly six-footers with a cute glare . . ."

(Bars crowded with customers, all staring up at the end of the bar, watching the fights on TV.)

"American Action Inc. is crawling out of its hole again, now that the war is safely won. What's the Inc. for, anyway? Incongruous? Incompetent? Incoherent? Or Ink-a-Dink-a-Doo? . . ."

Walter's voice is cut off abruptly as we see a man in his living room, surrounded by family and friends, unplug his radio. (We have seen this family before, in the montage sequence showing Walter's audience ten years before.) He replaces the radio plug with the plug of a television set, and the room fills with a cold blue light. They all stare into this light, as we see images from the early days of television: dancing cigarette packs, spark plugs performing close-order drill, Milton Berle in drag, Ed Sullivan announcing the guests on his show.

Walter is in his dressing room with a few Press Agents. They are watching Ed Sullivan on television. As Sullivan shtums and stammers and goes through his awkward mannerisms, Walter howls.

"Oy! Hey, Ma—tell 'em we don't want any!" He switches to a Bugs Bunny voice. "What a maroon . . . I'm laffin', I'm dyin' . . ."

"How long you give him, Walter?" a Press Agent says.

"He'll be lucky if they let him finish the hour," Walter says.

The Winchell column comes up. We see the title, "*Anniversary Song*." Walter's voice:

> *Ladies and Gentlemen*
> *(And Sour Grapers)*
> *This is my twenty-fourth Year*
> *On the papers.*
> *Greetings to Alla-Yez,*

(Cheerer and Jeerer)
This starts my nineteenth Year here,
On the Mirror.

Between the paragraphs of this column, we see the announcement, repeated: SEE WALTER WINCHELL ON ABC TV. CHANNEL 7, 6:45.

A television studio.
Walter is seated at a desk. We can see that he is wearing makeup. The microphone is overhead, but in every other detail, including the telegrapher's key, the desk is the same as the one used for his radio show. He is more nervous than usual. He stares uncomfortably at the cameras.
In the control room, the DIRECTOR flips a switch and calls down to his ASSISTANT on the floor.
"Ask him to please take his hat off."
Below, the assistant says to Walter, "Mr. Winchell, could we please see it without the hat?"
"I always wear a hat when I broadcast. It's my trademark."
"Well, men don't wear hats on television."
"Jimmy Durante wears a hat on television."
"*Tell* him to take it off," the director says.
"They say please take it off," the assistant says.
Peeved, Walter takes his hat off and drops it on the floor. The overhead lights hit his bald spot, creating a glare.
"Tell him to put his hat on," the director says.
"They say you can wear your hat, Mr. Winchell."

Over the opening announcements and credits of the first Winchell broadcast, we see Walter hitting the telegraph key. He's cued, and begins:
"Good evening, Mr. and Mrs. America and all the ships at

sea, this is Walter Winchell, an old newsboy in a new medium with items too rumorous to mention. I hope we'll be seeing a lot of each other. Let's go to press!

"Flash! Lana Turner won't start barking till she learns it here, but those delicious canapés served the other evening at the Scotty Fields' soirée were made from dog food.

"T. S. Eliot, St. Louis-born playwright, gave up his U.S. citizenship to become a Briddisher. His current Broadway click, *The Cocktail Party*, nets him three grand a week. He gave up everything American—except the money.

"Mrs. Horace Dodge is ill at Doctors Hospital in New York with malnutrition . . . And she's sooo rich.

"*Red Tide*, the new best-seller by Courtney Crew, documents Russia's plans for U.S. conquest. Read it and shiver . . ."

In a bar on Broadway, a bunch of Press Agents are watching the show.

"Down, boy, down," one of them says.

(And in fact there is something completely wrong with Walter Winchell on television. From the telegraph key to the hat, the effect is stiff, ridiculous. The lighting is brutal, making him look sinister. It's the kind of performance he used to give in vaudeville: overcooked, with no conviction. What the viewer sees, mostly, is an angry middle-aged man yelling at the camera.)

We hear one last item: "Ilsa Koch, the convicted Nazi monster, who bragged that she used the skin of concentration-camp victims to make lampshades, has had her life sentence cut to four years. . . . Oh, well . . . p'raps they were very small lampshades."

We see a series of headlines from *Variety*:

WINCHELL DEBUT SOLID RATINGS CLICK.

WINCHELL AUDIENCE DOWN.

WINCHELL DROPS OUT OF TOP 20. SULLIVAN NUMBER ONE FOR 39TH WEEK.

WINCHELL TELECAST CANCELED. VOWS WAR ON RATINGS.

Table 50, The Stork Club; Walter, Walda, and a YOUNG MAN. Walter is being extremely affable, playing the fond father to the room.

Dance floor; Walda and the young man are dancing, clearly in love.

We see Walter watching them now, far from affable, with a look that's positively venomous.

Walter's car, late at night. Walter is driving. Walda sits beside him.

"So what do we really know about this guy?" he says.

"Well, we know that I like him," Walda says.

"Like?"

"More than like. He's asked me to marry him."

Walter can barely keep his voice down. "Listen, baby, let me look into this guy, all right? If he checks out okay, we'll talk about it."

"Oh, Daddy, don't be silly. Billy's the sweetest boy I ever knew."

"Yeah? Then it won't hurt anything if I check him out. We'll find out how sweet. . . . Where was he during the war?"

"I don't know," Walda says. "He won't talk about it."

"I don't like this already," Walter says.

. . .

The house in Scarsdale. June and Walda.

Walda is in that state beyond tears, weak from her expended hysteria.

"Why are you doing this to us?" she asks June.

"Sweetie, your father knows what he's doing."

"He doesn't know a damned thing about Billy. He hasn't proven a single thing."

"Then how come Billy left town?" June says cautiously.

"And you're on his side!" Walda says. "You're *helping* him!"

"Baby, your father's only doing what he thinks is best for you."

Walda is suddenly dry and hard. "Really, Mother," she says. "How dumb can you get?"

In front of The Stork Club, after midnight. Walter is waiting as his car is brought around. He seems particularly alone.

A young man, BARRY GRAY, comes up to him.

"Mr. Winchell," he says.

Walter looks at him. "Who you?" he says.

"Barry Gray," the man says.

For a second, it's hard to know how he will react to being approached in this way. A flicker of suspicion, then he smiles.

"Well," he says. "Now I got a mug to put with the voice."

"Listen, I just wanted to say hello, and to thank you. You know, since you started plugging my program . . ."

"I know, I know, you've gone nowhere but up. You don't have to thank me, kid. I know big time when I hear it. Radio needs guys like you. You've got guts. So what are you doing?"

"You mean right now?"

"Yeah."

"Nothing. I was on my way home."

"Where do you live?"

"Uptown."

"I'm going uptown," Walter says. "I'll drop you off."

As they get into the car, Walter says, "You mind if we take the scenic route?"

Walter's car, driving at night.
Title Card: Autumn, 1951.

Walter broadcasting/the column:

"TIME MOTCHES ON!!! Little Margaret O'Brien has replaced the dollies at the head of her bed with a photo of Montgomery Clift . . .

"Hans Feurmann was finally found guilty this week of being a 'minor' Nazi . . . You know, folks . . . like a little garlic, or slightly pregnant . . . Ain't it a shame, Mame.

"Barry Gray's all-nighter was zippy and sassy yesterday ayem . . . Visiting West Coasters rate his microphone so highly he will probably be heard there soon . . .

"Doris Day's version of 'I Didn't Slip, I Wasn't Pushed, I Fell' is a melodic dimple . . . The sorta thing Edison had in mind when he invented the phonograph . . .

"Doc Kinsey's next bombshell will report that one-third of U.S. women sow wild oats before marriage . . ."

Three additional items are heard, over the following sequence:

Walter, at Table 50 with Irving Hoffman.

JOSEPHINE BAKER enters the Cub Room with a party of five, all Negroes. She and Walter spot each other across the room, smile warmly, and wave. But there is a surreal quality to this movement; it is repeated, as we hear Walter's voice:

"Josephine Baker, the American Negro star who has been the darling of Paris for twenty years, is due on our shores in a few weeks . . . She not only sings like a birdie and dances like an angel, but she has the courage of a lion. Only her extreme modesty has kept it a secret that Josie was a heroine of the French Resistance. Welcome home to a great lady . . .

"The ovation for Josephine Baker at the Ambassador could have gone on all night, but Josie stopped it herself, so she could resume knocking them dead . . .

"Josephine Baker has it all—class, talent, and ding-dong!"

On this line, the scene in the Cub Room becomes suddenly, clinically real; it moves into real time, and reveals some slight but sharp differences. Josephine Baker and Walter wave to each other, but we see, for example, that she is not particularly modest; she is somewhat arrogant, a very tough woman, and there is as much performance as warmth in her greeting.

As the MÂITRE D' leads her party to their table, she says, "I asked for something a little farther from the orchestra."

Table 50. Walter and Irving.

"That's a woman," Walter says.

"That's a colored woman," Irving says. "I can't wait to see Sherman's face."

"Are you kidding? Sherman knows she's here. He okayed it himself. Cover the phone, will you. I gotta go to a screening. Darryl's been hocking me to look at his picture all month."

He leaves.

Walter and Irving in Walter's car; night.

"So how was the picture?" Irving asks.

"I've seen better film on teeth," Walter says. He's fiddling with the radio dial. "Zanuck's so busy bending and stretching, he doesn't have time to make movies anymore . . . Shtup shtup shtup . . . Little cocker's this tall, and this long . . . See what my boy Barry's got tonight."

We hear the voice of Barry Gray on the car radio.

"But he was polite?"

"Oh, very polite," a woman's voice says. It is Josephine Baker. "I said, 'Listen, sugar, if there's one thing my people know how to be, it's patient.'"

"We're talking with Josephine Baker, ladies and gentlemen," Barry Gray says. "When you walked out of The Stork Club, no one said anything?"

"No."

"Or did anything?"

"Not a thing."

"These are pretty strong charges, Josephine. Walter Winchell has been a friend of mine for several years, and he's always fought bigotry of any kind."

"Well, he didn't fight it tonight in The Stork Club when I and my party were humiliated. Apparently his loyalty to Sherman Billingsley is greater than his loyalty to racial tolerance. . . ."

"Oy vey," Walter says.

Walter, in his office, on the phone with Barry Gray. We see both ends of the conversation.

"*Defend* myself!" Walter screams. "From what? I wasn't even there when it happened. *If* it happened. What, they had to wait half an hour to get served, what is the big frigging deal? Why the hell should I disgrace myself by defending myself. . . . Listen, kid, I never figured you for an ingrate."

"Oh, come on, Walter," Gray says. "You know damn well I'm grateful."

"Yeah, and you oughta be. I *made* you. Don't forget it."

"I don't forget. You helped me a lot, Walter. But what *made* me was an open microphone."

"You think so, shtunk? You watch. You watch. I'll close

your open microphone so frigging fast, you'll be talking into your *fist* when I'm through with you!"

He slams down the phone.

"Pisherke! I'll get *you.*"

He picks up the phone and dials.

"Listen, Barry Gray is *dead,* you got it? Move it around, and make sure everybody understands. Anybody who goes on his show is dead too . . . They want any of my ink, they leave that shlubb strictly alone."

He hangs up, redials.

"I want you to get busy for me on Barry Gray. Go back as far as you have to . . . a guy like that must have plenty to hide."

Night. The street in front of The Stork Club. There are a few pickets, carrying signs that read THE STORK CLUB DISCRIMINATES AGAINST NEGROES, JIM CROW MUST GO, etc. As Walter passes through them, they boo him.

Table 50. Walter and Sherman Billingsley.

"Listen, Sherm, you know I love a good brawl. I'm not happy unless I'm duking it out with somebody. But this thing is getting nuts. The NAACP will back us up one hundred percent if you'll give them a statement."

Billingsley smiles and looks around the room. "That Josephine Baker broad is certainly a pain in the ass," he says.

"You can say that again. But that's not the statement I had in mind. Those pinkos at the *Post* are already making this a megillah. And you know, it's amazing how many people there are with money who won't cross a picket line. This is making problems for both of us."

"Fuck 'em," Billingsley says. "They can't hurt us."

"Give 'em the statement, they'll stop trying."

"Listen, Walter. You know that I'd do almost anything for you. I'm in as deep as you are. But if I make this statement, they can start calling this place The Jigaboo Club. And that's never going to happen."

Walter looks down. "It's your place, Sherm," he says.

We see a New York *Post* headline: NAACP BOYCOTTS STORK.

We see the pickets in front of The Stork Club increased, as Walter broadcasts:

"Information made available to me indicates conclusively that the whole Josephine Baker–Stork Club tiff was stage-managed by the Communists. The object of this sordid exercise? What else? To embarrass and so silence this reporter. Your many letters and testimonials show me that only a few of you need reminding that the only color line I have ever drawn has been against those too yellow to tell the truth."

Walter, Table 50, hunched over a telephone.

"I don't get it. There's gotta be *something* on the guy. He's married ten years, and all he does is go home to his wife every night? Something stinks. Keep digging. Maybe he's a queer."

Lindy's; night. Walter enters, walks quickly toward his table. A MAN bumps into him.

"Excuse you," Walter says testily, not bothering to look at the man.

"You," the man says, recognizing Walter. "You ought to be ashamed of yourself."

"Sez who? Who the hell are *you*?"

"I'm just a guy who used to think you were pretty terrific," the man says, with more than a touch of self-righteousness.

"I read you every day for fifteen years. Now you're just another one of that bunch."

"And what bunch is this?" Walter says.

"You and that bum Billingsley. You got your noses so far up each other's ass you both smell like shit."

"Oh, yeah?" Walter says, shoving the man. The man shoves back, hard. Walter stumbles against his table. He grabs the ketchup bottle and throws it. It strikes the man, breaks. The man sags, groggy, and goes down, covered in ketchup.

Walter stands over him, shaking with rage. He pulls out his gun.

"You're lucky, you bastard," he yells. "I could have used *this* on you!"

He sticks the gun back in his pocket and leaves Lindy's.

We see Barry Gray paying off a taxi. As he walks up the street, two men grab him, shove him against a wall, and beat him up.

(Over this, Walter's voice: "Borey Pink—I mean Barry Gray's agents can't get anyone to take him. They've offered all kinds of concessions in vain. The has-been even offered to work for nothing, and they gave him that Get-Lost Glare.")

The Stork Club; Table 50. Walter, on the phone: "He thinks *I* had it done? That's nuts. . . . Probably somebody trying to get on my good side. . . . Yeah, and they did a lousy job, too. The punk's still walking around. With no place to go."

We see that several changes have been made in the Cub Room. A glass partition has been installed, separating the tables from the orchestra and dance floor. It isolates the table, causing changes in the light and atmosphere of the space. Where it was exclusive before, it's claustrophobic now.

Sitting in Damon Runyon's old spot beside Walter is a repellent young man with slick black hair, shifty but sharp eyes, and a faint involuntary sneer almost always on his face; ROY COHN. He is a congenital conspirator. His mouth is glued to a spot two inches from Walter's ear, he speaks low but intensely while his eyes make a lazy sweep of the room, inviting attention while guarding against eavesdroppers.

For once, Walter is nearly silent. He's also upset. The conversation is obviously frightening him. As he listens, he tears off bits of bread and rolls them into little pills with his fingers.

"I don't want there to be any misunderstanding," Cohn is saying. "The McCarthy Committee obviously knows you're not a Communist, or a Communist sympathizer, or anything of the kind."

"I should hope they know it," Walter says. "I've been fighting those bastards for twenty-five years."

"The Senator isn't so sure about your friend Drew Pearson."

"Aw, Drew's okay," Walter says meekly.

"Maybe he is," Cohn says. "But I don't think you want to say that publicly right now."

"No?" Walter tries to sound tough.

"No. We're investigating him. And there are a few people who think we should be investigating you."

"Me?" Walter says. He flicks one of the little bread pills at the floor. A WAITER, standing nearby, picks it up. Walter sees this out of the corner of his eye, and smiles to himself.

"You were running pro-Russian items as late as 1947," Cohn says.

"We were at war!"

"Not in 1947, we weren't."

"After the war, all *we* wanted to do with the Nazis and the Japs was kiss and make up. The Russians wanted to hang the bastards. You're a kid, Roy. You don't know what was going on here. You've got to remind them. You've got to tell them."

"I'm only the lawyer, Walter. I can't tell the Senator what to do. Joe does what he wants. And frankly, he's very disappointed in New York in general and you in particular. We're not getting the kind of support we expected from the papers here. Some of the responses have been downright hostile."

"Well, the *Post*, sure," Walter says. "The *Post* is as pink as a flamingo's asshole. I mean, look at the way they backed up that meshuggeneh Baker broad. Not that it did her any good . . ."

He makes a sudden wild, desperate stab at intimacy with Cohn.

"Ernest Hemingway told me he laid her in Paris. . . . Well, not exactly laid her, they did it standing up. . . . He said she was like an animal."

Walter might as well be sharing this with a stone. Cohn's manner and expression don't change. Walter fires off a second bread pill. The Waiter picks it up. Walter smiles directly at him.

"And you know, Roy, Sherman was right about that business . . . Two–three weeks, everybody forgot."

"Not everybody," Cohn says. "We saw very clearly how the lines got drawn. A lot of people tipped their hand. The same people that are against us are against you. We're against the same people you're against. So how come you aren't for us?"

"But I *am* for you!" Walter says.

"Then it wouldn't hurt anything if you'd say so."

Walter looks at the Waiter and flicks another pill. The Waiter doesn't move.

"Hey," Walter yells. "What're you getting paid for?"

"Not for this, Mr. Winchell," the Waiter says.

"Oh, no? You're fired, mister."

"I don't work for you, Mr. Winchell."

"That's what *you* think, shmuckola."

The people at the nearest table have turned to watch this scene.

"What do *you* want?" Walter yells at them. "Look someplace else or I'll have you thrown out."

Headline, New York *Post*: WW ADMITS: REDS USED ME.

We see newsreel footage of Joseph McCarthy.

Over this, Walter broadcasting:

"Senator Joseph McCarthy is preparing a new and long list of Red Spies. Local ComRats are plenty nervous.

"Joe McCarthy's forthcoming revelations about Scummunist infiltration into the highest levels of U.S. Army Command will be a bombshell . . . Watch this space!

"For those who claim that I used to be a little pink, the only red that's ever been in my heart has always been accompanied by white and blue . . ."

Lindy's, night. The Press Agents, Irving.

First P.A.: "Does he know what the hell he's talking about?"

Second P.A.: "Somebody ought to tell him to calm down."

First P.A.: "Good idea. *You* tell him."

Second P.A.: "Maybe I will. You think I'm afraid of him? People are getting good and fed up. He's not going to be any good to any of us. That Barry Gray business left a bad taste."

Third P.A.: "It shouldn't have happened to a dog."

Second P.A.: "It's degrading to our profession."

Fourth P.A.: "To our *wha?*"

Second P.A.: "I'm serious. My grandfather fought with Garibaldi."

First P.A.: "Yeah? What was the beef?"

"Forget it," Irving says. "He'll jump off the McCarthy band-wagon long before it hits the wall."

Second P.A.: "You think so? I don't think he's smart enough."

"What, smart?" Irving says. "He'll get bored."

We see various shots of the New York *Post* REPORTERS crank-ing up and pursuing their investigation.

We see them leave the *Post* building, get into a car. We see them talking or trying to talk to various people: PRESS AGENTS, EMILE GAUVREAU, WALTER'S SECRETARY, ED SULLIVAN, WOLFIE, The Stork Club WAITER that Walter had fired, etc.

We see a layout table, with photos of Walter.

We see a researcher poring over old Winchell columns, circling various items in red.

Over the *Post* montage, Walter broadcasts:

"When the Duke and Duchess of Windsor visited Wash-ington last week, the only celeb they wanted to dine with was Senator Joseph McCarthy. The social climbers!"

"Great advice to young writers from Ernest Hemingway: 'Never pay attention to the critics. If you believe them when they tell you you're good, then you have to believe them when they tell you you're bad.'

"The new editor of *Pravda* is Dmitri Trafimovich Shepilov. It's logical that a guy with a name like that should be in charge of twisting the Truth."

We see the *Post* team typing.

The researcher has compiled a long list of circled items. On the top, in red, he writes, WW'S WRONGOS.

The photos spread over the layout desk show Walter with Billingsley, J. Edgar Hoover, Frank Costello, etc.

Lindy's, night. The Press Agents.
First P.A.: "I don't know. . . . You're starting to look a little pink to me."
Third P.A.: "It must be the borscht."
First P.A.: "Those guys from the *Post* talk to you?"
Third P.A. (Cagey, evasive): "What guys?"
Second P.A.: "Yeah, they talked to you. What did you tell them?"
Third P.A.: "I told them that Walter Winchell is my closest personal friend and the greatest newspaperman in America."
First P.A.: "Me too. I hope they really give it to that prick."

Walter, broadcasting:
"A little birdie tells me that the New York *Compost*, a so-called newspaper in our town, is preparing a series of articles about your newsboy. It will, naturally, be a hatchet job, because they know that I stand for everything they are most afraid of. And what do they fear the most? The Truth. No man can ever qualify as an American journalist unless his North Star is the Truth. Well, go ahead with your little hatchets. You may get me, but you will never chop down the Tree of Truth. It will dwarf you. This is Walter Winchell in New York, reminding you that if you have Communism in your mind, you cannot have America in your heart."

Office of the publisher, the New York *Post*.
The Reporters, DOROTHY SCHIFF, JAMES WECHSLER. The series is on Dorothy Schiff's desk.
"There's enough for at least twenty articles," she says.

"He'll fight back," Wechsler says. "Nobody's ever dared touch him before."

"Let him," Schiff says. "We'll sell papers."

"Oh, we'll sell papers. But if you fight with Winchell, you have to fight in the sewer. It's the only way with that guy."

"I remember when we were on the same side," Schiff says. She hands the articles to the reporters. "Run this through Legal. I want to start as soon as possible."

We see the New York *Post* delivery truck, carrying a large advertisement. The elements are a photo of Walter, a keyhole, a set of gleaming keys. The copy reads: INSIDE WINCHELL. THE MAN—THE GHOSTS—THE REAL STORY . . . BEGINNING MONDAY IN THE NEW YORK POST.

A montage of successive issues of the New York *Post*, headlines: WALTER WINCHELL, THE HOLLOW MAN . . . WINCHELL'S NUMBER ONE GHOST . . . WINCHELL AND THE MOB . . . WINCHELL AND MCCARTHY . . . WALTER MAKES A STAR . . . THE WINCHELL FIRING SQUAD. Each article contains a box, filled with items from the Winchell column, headed WW's WRONGOS.

We see the *Post* being snapped up at the newsstands, being read on the subway, talked about, etc. We see one of the Press Agents draw the curtains in his hotel room and carefully take the *Post* out of a pile of papers. He begins reading it, enjoying himself tremendously.

The Stork Club, dance floor. Roy Cohn is dancing with a pretty young woman. Mutual distaste radiates from both. Through the partition next to Table 50, Walter watches them like a kid with his nose to the glass. He's alone.

Sherman Billingsley slides in next to him.

"You know," he says, "your friends are always welcome here."

"I should hope so," Walter says.

"But *him*, me no like," Billingsley says, nodding toward Cohn. "It's incredible how many of the people who come in here feel the same way."

"Let 'em go to Schrafft's then."

"Absolutely, Walter, to Schrafft's with them. But man to man, you be careful with these guys. They're going down, and they'll take you with them."

He stands.

"If Damon was around, he'd tell you the same thing," he says. He notices a spot on the back of the banquette, and leans over to brush it.

"What the hell does he put on his hair?" he says.

The Winchell column hits the screen like a barrage. We hear Walter reading one item:

"The execution of convicted red spies Julius and Ethel Rosenberg has been set for January 14th. That's appropriate . . . January 14th is the birthday of America's number one traitor, Benedict Arnold."

Lindy's, late night. Walter is sitting with Irving Hoffman.

As Walter talks, he jabs his finger at the table. "You bet I hate the Rosenbergs. I hate 'em because they're Commies, I hate 'em because they're spies, and most of all, I hate 'em because they're Jews. They're the greatest ad for anti-Semitism since Georgie Jessel, and look who's crying for them—Jews. Oh, the poor, poor Rosenbergs. My piles really bleed for them."

"This is a tough time," Irving says. He's clearly got a lot on his mind.

"Nah. They been kicking me in the slats for twenty-five years, and all it's gotten them is sore toes. Hmpf! Finger-snap in face!" He snaps his fingers. "Besides, they're just using my name to sell papers."

"Well, they're selling a lot of them," Irving says. "Most of the flak you're getting is coming from people who used to be your friends."

"Times change," Walter says. "And all their highfalutin ideals, it sure doesn't stop them from attacking *my* politics."

Irving laughs. "Aw, come on, Walter, you haven't *got* any politics. Showmanship, you got. Nerve ends, you got plenty. They're right out there now flapping in the breeze. You ought to pull them in a little before they break off."

Walter seems confused. "Is that what you think, Irving?"

"As a friend. A lot of people think so who aren't so friendly. They're saying you can dish it out, but you can't take it."

"Take it!" Walter yells. "Why on earth should *I* have to *take* it? You're telling me this as a *friend*? Some friend . . . some frigging friend *you* are."

"Walter, please . . ."

But Walter is out of control. "You were a big help with Barry Gray! I told you to stop Danny Kaye from going on that punk's show . . ."

"Danny's a big boy. Nobody tells him what to do."

"After what I did for Danny . . . and *you*! Jesus, I can't believe you're with *them* . . ."

"Listen, we'll talk later," Irving says, leaving.

"The hell we will! Drop dead!"

Walter glares after Irving. The waiter comes by.

"Something else, Walter?"

"Yeah. Bring me some Scotch tape. I want to lengthen my list of ingrates!"

A dark city street. The wind blows newspapers up the street, so many of them that you can't be sure whether it's a dream or not.

Walter's voice, broadcasting. It's weak, on the verge of breaking:

"But I don't mind . . . I don't mind them throwing mud at me . . . It's the same mud they've been dragging America through for years . . ."

We see a notice in the *Mirror*, in place of the column: *Walter Winchell's physicians have ordered him to take an immediate rest from all activities. He hopes to resume shortly.*

Miami. The front of the Roney Plaza Hotel.

Walter, singing to himself, to the tune of "It Might As Well Be Spring":

> *I'm as lonely as a gentile at the Roney,*
> *I'm as jumpy as a bubke on a string . . .*

He enters the apartment, greets June with a kiss. We see that she's been drinking; that she drinks all the time.

"Where's Junior?" Walter says.

"He went to the beach with some friends."

"Jesus, I can never talk to that kid. Even when he's here, it doesn't make any difference. Can *you* talk to him?"

"It ain't easy," June says.

"Walda call?"

"Yes."

"And."

"No dice."

"Jesus, she's stubborn."

"My side of the family, no doubt," June says. "Give it some time. She's hurt."

"Hurt—what? I should have just let her marry that bum? So he could live off my name? That would have been some addition to the family."

"I tell her you were looking out for her."

"Yeah? And what did *she* say?" Walter says, as though it's a vaudeville feed line.

"What do you think she says? By the way, that no good momser Irving Hoffman called." (She says this with affection.)

"What the hell did *he* want?"

"He wanted to know how you are."

"He's got a nerve. . ."

"He's the best friend you've got."

"Sherman's the best friend I've got."

"Then God help you."

"Sherm never stabbed me in the back."

"Oh baloney. Irving didn't stab you in the back or anywhere else. Anyway, he's in Miami for ten days. What's the matter? Afraid to say you were wrong?"

"I'm not afraid of anything or anyone," Walter says. "Except you, doll. I'm scared to death of you."

He rests his head on June's breast; they're more like child and mother than husband and wife.

A practice green, Miami. Irving Hoffman, all dressed up for golf, makes a few myopic putts. They all miss the cup.

Walter approaches.

"Damon used to say that the only thing about golf that requires courage is the clothes," Walter says.

Irving squints.

"Listen, Irving, I'm truly sorry. Can't we be friends?"

"So what else could we be?" Irving says.

Walter hugs Irving, then bursts into tears.

A Miami nightclub. Walter, June, and Irving are finishing dinner. Walter looks over at June's plate. She's left a bit of food. He spears it with his fork.

"I can't stand to see food go to waste," he says.

"Think of all the starving press agents in China," Irving says.

"You never know, Oiving."

A time lapse of several minutes.

"I don't know what you keep knocking yourself out for," Irving says. "Why don't you just write a book?"

"A whole book?" Walter says.

"Yeah. Write your autobiography. It'd sell a million."

"Aw, I could never tell the truth about myself," Walter says. "Besides, I gotta get the column out. The war's not over. I better get back before they forget me."

While Irving and June give each other a sad look, Walter laughs weakly.

Walter, back in New York, broadcasting:

"James Wechsler may be more familiar to his old friends as Arthur Lawson—the name he used when he was an official of the Young Communists League, and under which he once renounced his country. His early training in treason, treachery, and lies made him the ideal choice for the job he holds today—editor-in-chief of the New York *Post* . . ."

.   .   .

The office of a NETWORK EXECUTIVE. Walter, Walter's LAW-YER, the EXECUTIVE, Walter's PRODUCER, and the network's NEWS DIRECTOR.

"Walter, the New York *Post* is suing us," the Exec says.

"Oh boy!" Walter says, thrilled.

"I'm afraid we don't share your enthusiasm," the Exec says.

"But don't you get it?" Walter says. "This means I've *won*!"

"It means, I'm afraid, that you've made some extremely reckless charges against the paper and its editor and publisher."

"No, no, no . . . Newspapermen are supposed to fight each other without running to lawyers. These bastards are licked, believe me."

"In any case, this network categorically refuses to continue carrying the full legal burden for every damned thing you happen to feel like saying about anyone."

"Oh yeah?" Walter says. He turns to the Producer and the Director. "Is that how you boys feel?"

At the same moment, one of them says "Yes," the other says "No."

"You should hold a rehearsal," Walter says.

"Fortunately, Walter," the Lawyer says, "they'll settle for a retraction."

"A retraction. I'll give them a frigging retraction. . . ."

"Then we'll give them one," the Exec says.

"You do, you can kiss me goodbye," Walter says, walking out of the office. The Lawyer makes a placatory gesture and follows him.

"He doesn't get it at all, does he?" the Exec says.

Late night, Walter's office. He's on the telephone.

"Listen, when I want your advice, I'll ask for it. . . . Okay, okay, I'm sorry . . . I *know* I did. . . . I *know* you're my lawyer. They'll back down like they always do. No, this is about my journalistic principles. . . . You watch. I already sent them my letter of resignation."

We see the Lawyer now, in his bathrobe, exasperated. "That's what I've been trying to tell you, Walter. It's been accepted."

Walter, in close-up, shocked, bewildered. "What, you mean just like that?" His voice cracks. "I'll have to call you back."

He puts the phone down quietly.

"Boom!" he says. "Just like that."

The camera moves across the map of the United States on the wall of Walter's office, with its thousand flags. In a series of slow dissolves, we see the number of flags decreasing, from a thousand to less than two hundred.

We hear, then see, the Press Agents.

First P.A.: "They don't give a shit anymore. The new kids I'm getting today don't care whether I get them into Winchell or not. They'd rather see their names in Lyons. . . ."

Second P.A.: "It's certainly a pleasure doing business with Lyons. A real gentleman."

Third P.A.: "I'd rather deal with Dorothy Kilgallen than Walter."

Second P.A.: "You go too far."

First P.A.: "You know what I heard? I heard when all those papers dropped his column they didn't get one letter. Not even a How Come."

Third P.A.: "Barry Gray's back in business."

Fourth P.A.: "He's bigger than ever. And there wasn't a frigging thing Walter could do about it, either."

First P.A.: "Boy, I bet that got him good and crazy. . . ."

Second P.A.: "We still kiss his ass."

First P.A.: "Habit. We been doing it for so long we don't

even know we're doing it. . . . Besides, he's still got two hundred papers. That's not applesauce."

Fourth P.A.: "And he's still on the air coast-to-coast."

Second P.A.: "Coast-to-coast—New York and L.A., coast-to-coast."

Third P.A.: "You know, I feel sorry for the guy. He seems so fermischt."

First P.A.: "Geddaddahere, sorry for him. He's a rotten human being. I mean, look at his family. . . ."

Third P.A.: "Oh come on . . ."

First P.A.: "His mother jumped out a window. His wife's a drunk. That sweet little girl of his goes around crying all the time. And Junior's a Looney Toone. He's even crazier than his father."

Coming out of this, we see Walter Winchell, Jr., walking down Third Avenue, late afternoon. He's dressed in the uniform of an officer of the Waffen S.S., a horrible, arrogant sneer on his face.

He enters a bar. The people inside look at him in that New York way, like they've seen it all before but they don't want to be seeing it right now.

He swaggers to the bar, removes his hat and gloves, places them on the bar, and speaks to the BARTENDER.

"A double. At once."

"A double what?" the Bartender says, with great hostility.

"Don't trouble me with details," Walter Jr. says.

The Bartender pours a double shot of the bar rye. Walter Jr. lifts the drink, looks around the room.

"To the Führer!" he says, and downs the drink. He puts the glass down, snaps his fingers at the Bartender.

"Listen," the Bartender says, "drink someplace else. I lost a lot of buddies fighting shit like you."

"I hope they appreciated the privilege," Walter Jr. says.

"Hey. Fuck you."

"Fuck *me?*" Walter Jr. says. "No no no. Fuck *you.*"

He takes a bottle from the bar, smashes it, and jams it into the Bartender's face.

The house in Scarsdale. Walter, June, and Walter Jr. June has been crying.

"Listen," Walter says, "we're not mad at you . . ."

"Not *mad* at me?" Walter Jr. says, laughing.

"We just want to know why you did it. I mean, what the *hell* kind of *crazy cockamamy* way is *that* to act!?"

Walter Jr. smiles. "Just ask yourself—how would *you* act if you had Walter Winchell for a father?"

The lobby of The Stork Club.

Two of the Press Agents are standing near the hatcheck counter. One of them is on the phone, the other is twirling his hat on his finger. They hear Walter shouting as he leaves the Cub Room, "Find yourself another stairway to the stars!"

Walter walks quickly past the photographs on the wall. He stops in front of his own, pulls it from the wall, and tucks it under his arm.

"That hillbilly is through using my name to fill his joint every night," he says. He motions angrily for his hat, grabs it, and leaves.

"Well, I guess that makes everybody now," one of the Press Agents says.

"No," the other one says. "He hasn't had a fight with Mother Cabrini yet."

We see the bare spot on The Stork Club wall left by Walter's picture. A title card: Autumn, 1960.

We see Billingsley personally polishing the frame before returning it.

Time lapse. Night, The Stork Club.

Walter and Sherman enter the Cub Room together, arms around each other's shoulders. Nobody notices them. They go to Table 50.

The crowd in the Cub Room seems mostly made up of tourists: conventioneers, small-town retailers. The former convivial hum has been replaced by the sound of people who talk and laugh too loud; crude drinkers and exhibitionists. White socks are perfectly acceptable. The waiters aren't as sharp as they were. The jackets are a shade or two short of white; one waiter shows a heavy five-o'clock shadow. The cigarette girl looks and acts like a tart. The famous lighting has lost all its tone, without anybody noticing. The orchestra has shrunk to a combo, playing "Three Coins in the Fountain."

Walter and Billingsley, Table 50.

"You know who came in here last night?" Billingsley says. "You remember Biddy Rawlings?"

"Remember her?" Walter says. "I got her jewelry back for her when she was robbed at the Colony. I put it on the air, and next morning we had the stuff. . . . She still a lush?"

"Nope. She hasn't had a drink in years. She's about the only one of that bunch that straightened herself out. Trudie Drexel was still coming in here, until I had her barred."

"Drunk?"

"Not only drunk. She wet her pants in here."

Walter laughs.

"It's not funny. I had to have the whole banquette re-covered. It cost me two hundred bucks."

"Two hundred bucks? I remember when you thought hundred-dollar bills were for filling balloons with."

"That was before the unions got me by the balls. . . . Jack Kennedy made a reservation a few nights ago, but he never showed."

"He's busy," Walter says.

"You think he'll make it?"

"I don't know. . . . Now that people vote with their genitals, anything can happen. Imagine, a little pisherke like that . . . rich kid. I've seen a million of 'em. Playboy, fucking everything with a wiggle . . ."

"He was a war hero," Billingsley says.

"He's lucky he didn't get court-martialed . . . Joe's money."

Billingsley looks around the room with contempt.

"Now we get this," he says. "Different type of crowd altogether."

"They're spending," Walter says.

"Yeah, they are, and even their money is boring. There's no nightlife anymore. Television killed it . . . the unions killed it. . . ."

"Café society wasn't so hot, either," Walter says. "You forget, Sherm . . . half of them ended up in the toilet. They were pimping, they were blackmailing, God knows what . . . Damon used to say that their fathers left them a mint instead of a mind. They just pissed it away."

"I know. But when they first started coming in here . . ."

"Aw, they were lost the first time they got their pictures in the paper."

"But it was great to have them in the room. They drank me out of house and home. They were a pain in the ass. But God, they were gorgeous."

. . .

The sidewalk in front of the New York *Mirror*, afternoon. The building's entrance is blocked by strike pickets. Walter fights his way through.

"Hey, Walter, ain't you with us?" a picket calls.

"With you?" Walter snarls. "You destroyed this newspaper! You murdered half the papers in New York! With you? You oughta be killed!"

The crowd mutters, "Old cocker," "Fascist prick."

Walter's office. Walter and his SECRETARY.

Movers are taking down the map. Boxes filled with photographs, etc.

"Well," Walter says. "They sank my flagship."

"At least we've got a paper to go to," the Secretary says.

"That's 'cause I'm a headliner, kid. There's no time like the big time."

Walter's office at the *Journal-American*.

It's small, crowded with unpacked boxes. The map is on the floor, resting against the wall. Walter is typing. We hear the sound of typing throughout the following sequence.

We see the *Journal-American* column. The large type and new format only point up the thinness of it; and the fact that it's barely a quarter of its old length. The ink sketch of Walter above the column shows an old man. We hear various items spoken by Walter in a travesty of excitement and energy:

"Many dopes who think they are getting high on marijuana are being sold oregano, which has no effect . . .

"Gina Lollobrigida never wears a girdle . . .

"Most people who wear dark specs at night give themselves away. Dark specs invariably mark the Phony, the Pusher, the Addict, the Prosty, and the Creepnik . . .

"Russia's favorite cosmonaut is ill: gets dizzy spells, keeps falling down . . .

"The Beatles should clip and save this reminder: Whatever happened to some RockenRollers who had crowds of mental cripples swooning? The one-hit-record army of no-talents. . . ."

"This reporter has received conclusive evidence that Ernest Hemingway's death was not a suicide, as many people believe . . ."

Walter, typing, in his office. The map is still leaning against the wall. His desk is crowded with Christmas presents.

A few YOUNG REPORTERS stop in.

"Hey, Walter, we're going out to get loaded. Wanna come?"

"If you were going out to get laid, I might join you . . . Gotta get the column out . . . you know, it never stops . . ." He types a little burst. "Same old Winchell, hey, fellas?"

"Yeah," one of them says with obvious mockery. "I don't know how you do it."

They walk away laughing, but Walter doesn't hear.

Night. Walter is sitting at his desk, depressed, staring at the Christmas presents. The phone rings, he picks it up.

"Yowza . . . No. You want the Sports Desk." He holds his nose and talks like a New York operator in a comedy sketch: "No, I cannot connect you . . . I am *not* the frigging operator."

He hangs up. The phone rings again.

"Hello . . . Hiya, doll . . . Yeah, I'll be home in a few hours. I'm going by the Palace and give Billy Conti a hand . . . I've been helping them with their show . . . Walk out and do five minutes . . . Yeah. They're tickled to death. Okay, maw. I love you, baby."

He hangs up. He picks up a Christmas present, stares at it, and lets it drop onto the desk.

. . .

A dressing room, the Palace Theatre. A fat comic, BILLY CONTI, is stuffing a pastrami sandwich into his face.

The STAGE MANAGER comes in.

"Winchell's out there again," he says.

"Oh, no," Conti says. "That fuckin' pest. I'll take care of him for good."

Onstage, the Palace. Walter has his arm around TONY DRAPER, a crooner, and is trying to walk him through a soft-shoe routine, clearly against Draper's will. The crooner is almost deranged with a combination of rage and embarrassment.

"God," Walter is saying, "they don't teach you kids anything. Look, it's a-one-two-three, bump; one-two-three, turn. Can you walk, Tony? Okay, professor, if I could have a little 'Jimmy Valentine' . . . a number that I almost buried on this very stage . . . never mind when."

The audience is as embarrassed as the crooner. As the orchestra pulls together something resembling "Jimmy Valentine," Billy Conti walks onstage.

He smiles at the audience and hugs Walter. Out of the corner of his mouth, he says, "We happen to be booked into this theatre right now. I hear the Automat's looking for talent."

Walter freezes, then turns on Conti. "Why you little putz, I was in this game before you were born."

The first few rows pick this up.

Billy Conti smiles to the audience. "He used to work with that old Chinese vaudeville act, On Too Long."

This gets a laugh.

"You all remember Walter Winchell, ladies and gentlemen

. . . Good evening, Mr. and Mrs. America, and all the ships
at sea? Remember that? . . . No? I don't think they remember,
Walter."

"I remember when you used to sleep outside my door to
get your name in my column . . . The first time I saw your
act, you hadn't even heard of your*self.*"

"He used to be the Lion of Broadway, people. But now he's
just an old pussycat. Here, puddy, puddy, puddy . . ."

The audience laughs.

Walter walks off the stage, as the comic and the crooner
work up applause for him.

Walter leaves the Palace to wander in a ghost world. The
old bunch that used to hang out in front of the Palace give
him that "Gee, it's great to see you down" laugh, and are
gone. We see for the first time how old Walter really is. He's
like a ghost himself.

We see Times Square and Forty-second Street, circa 1965.

Walter drives late at night through a hostile and dangerous
Harlem.

Lindy's, night. Walter sits alone.

Several tables away, a few Press Agents are seated.

"Here, puddy puddy puddy," one of them says.

"Hey!" Walter yells. "I *heard* that!"

"Yeah?" the Press Agent says. "Good. I'm glad. I thought
you were deaf, you crazy old bastard. Goddamn crazy old
man."

Walter smiles, sticks his thumb to his nose, and wiggles his
fingers, like the kid in the School Days act.

Walter sits at home with June, watching a rerun of *The*

Untouchables. He's thrilled by the sound of his voice on the soundtrack.

Walter, sitting alone, unnoticed in the busy lobby of a hotel. He wanders in and out of clubs.

The camera moves down the street and stops in front of The Stork Club. There is a locked iron grate across the door. The awning is torn and filthy. Clumps of old newspapers are piled against the grate. The club is dark. On the grate is a sign:

STORK CLUB CLOSED. WILL RELOCATE.

We hear what sounds like a small waterfall. From Walter's p.o.v. we see the crowds in the Cub Room of The Stork Club, circa 1943, turning in response to the force of energy at their backs; they smile in recognition, some of them saying hello. We see Table 50, with Runyon, Billingsley, and Hemingway, smiling in greeting. They speak, but we can't hear them.

Then we see Walter, an old and nearly broken man, walking slowly through the Cub Room toward the table.

We cut abruptly to the small waterfall at the rear of Paley Park, a vest-pocket park in the place where The Stork Club once stood. Walter, alone and unrecognized, is sitting at a table, amid shoppers with parcels and office workers eating their lunch.

Walter and June enter a restaurant. In the foyer, they run into Ed Sullivan and his WIFE. Walter is touchingly hesitant to speak to him.

"Look who it is," Sullivan says to his wife. She and June embrace.

"Hiya, Ed," Walter says, shyly. "It's great to see you."

"You too," Ed says, giving Walter a hug.

"You look just the same," he says.

"So do you," Walter says. "You never change. I've known Ed for forty years, and he always looked old."

They all laugh.

"I'm still growing," Walter says, removing his hat to show his baldness. "Look . . . my head's pushed its way up through my hair . . . Seventy years old, last week."

"Go on . . ."

"And you heard it here first!"

"Well, that doesn't mean it's true," Sullivan says.

"Aw, you're still a son-of-a-bitch," Walter says.

We see the four of them seated on a banquette. June motions to the club photographer.

"We've got to get a picture of this," she says.

Ed and Walter hug each other and smile at the camera, a couple of tough, scarred survivors.

The flash goes off, the frame freezes, becomes a photograph on a wall.

It's one of hundreds of photographs that cover one wall of a long corridor: pictures of Walter at various stages in his life. He's seen with presidents, movie stars, athletes; photos of Walter in jokey love clinches with actresses; delivering a gag knockout punch to heavyweight champions. We see him with Roosevelt, Billingsley, Runyon, Hoover, Costello. We see the photograph that hung for so many years in The Stork Club.

A shimmering piano plays "Autumn in New York." We hear faraway noises of New York: traffic, silverware on china, glasses clinking, laughter.

·   ·   ·

We see a stretch of Arizona desert: giant cacti, scrub desert, clean thin early-morning light. A large house, with a pool and a flagpole; the sounds of New York continue.

Walter, asleep in his bedroom. He wakes up, and the New York noises stop.

We see Walter, dressed in an expensive silk bathrobe, walking down the hall past the photographs. He sticks his head in the den. There's no one there, but the television set is on. Richard Nixon is on the screen.

"Still foolin' 'em, hey, shmuckelheimer?" Walter says to the screen.

He steps to a large picture window. Out on the lawn an INDIAN TEENAGER is waiting by the flagpole with a folded American flag. Walter waves a signal to him, the boy waves back, and starts to fix the flag to the rope.

We hear the Press Agents talking against this.

First P.A.: "I hated the fucking guy. He was like a little gray mouse, always sniffing around for cheese. Whaddya got, whaddya got? . . ."

Second P.A.: "A mouse? A rat."

Third P.A.: "He was, he was a real rat. But I liked him."

First P.A.: "You're a masochist."

Third P.A.: "Maybe, but I miss him. I miss Irving, too."

Second P.A.: "Irving, God bless him. He's gone to a better place."

First P.A.: "Yeah. L.A."

We see them now, in Lindy's. Max, the old waiter, is filling their cups.

First P.A.: "I bet Maxie misses Walter's tips."

The old waiter smiles, shrugs, as if to say, "I don't miss his tips, but I miss him."

First P.A.: "The last of the ten-cent tippers."

Third P.A.: "And with his dough . . ."

First P.A.: "Walter was so tight he took his glasses off when he wasn't looking at anything."

Third P.A.: "Did you ever see him cry?"

First P.A.: "No. And I used to ask God every night to let me see that."

Third P.A.: "Jesus, he cried at the drop of a hat."

First P.A.: "It's only fair."

Second P.A.: "Say what you want, the town isn't the same without him. The whole game's changed. It's worse."

We see the Indian teenager now, but hear the last few lines of the Press Agents.

Third P.A.: "I had this package of Japanese movies I was pushing, and I went to him, and he started with 'They bombed our boys! They bombed our boys!' I said, 'Walter, don't be such a shmuck—twenty-five years ago they bombed our boys.' "

Second P.A.: "You said that?"

Third P.A.: "Well . . . I thought it."

The Indian teenager waves again to Walter. Walter pushes a little button on the wall, and the flag automatically starts up the pole.

Walter stands at attention, grabs his balls, and salutes.

We see the flag flying in the desert wind; tumbleweed blows by, and with it, the last few phrases of "Autumn in New York."

. . .

The spot by the picture window where Walter stood a moment before. He's gone.

We see him walking away from us down the long hallway in his bathrobe; receding.

We hear the voice of the young Walter Winchell, singing "America, I love you, you're like a sweetheart of mine," as the closing credits come up.

A NOTE ON THE TYPE

This book was set in Electra, a type face designed by W(illiam) A(ddison) Dwiggins (1880–1956) for the Mergenthaler Linotype Company and first made available in 1935. Electra cannot be classified as either "modern" or "old style." It is not based on any historical model, and hence does not echo any particular period or style of type design. It avoids the extreme contrast between thick and thin elements that marks most modern faces, and it is without eccentricities that catch the eye and interfere with reading. In general, Electra is a simple, readable type face that attempts to give a feeling of fluidity, power, and speed.

W. A. Dwiggins was born in Martinsville, Ohio, and studied art in Chicago. In the late 1920s he moved to Hingham, Massachusetts, where he built a solid reputation as a designer of advertisements and as a calligrapher. He began an association with the Mergenthaler Linotype Company in 1929 and over the next 27 years designed a number of book types of which Metro, Electra, and Caledonia have been used widely.

Composed by Crane Typesetting Service, Inc.,
West Barnstable, Massachusetts
Printed and bound by Fairfield Graphics,
Fairfield, Pennsylvania
Designed by Virginia Tan